D0344068

EYE OF THE SUN

Also by Dianne Hofmeyr

FISH NOTES AND STAR SONGS
EYE OF THE MOON

EYE OF THE SUN

DIANNE HOFMEYR

SIMON AND SCHUSTER

For Phillip

SIMON AND SCHUSTER
First published in Great Britain in 2008
by Simon and Schuster UK Ltd, a CBS company.

Copyright © 2008 Dianne Hofmeyr
Map copyright © 2007 Simon and Schuster

The right of Dianne Hofmeyr to be identified as
the author of this work has been asserted by her in
accordance with sections 77 and 78 of the Copyright,
Design and Patents Act, 1988.

Simon & Schuster UK Ltd
Africa House, 64–78 Kingsway, London WC2B 6AH.

A CIP catalogue record for this book is available
from the British Library.

ISBN: 978-1-41691-128-9

10 9 8 7 6 5 4 3 2 1

Typeset by Rowland Phototypesetting Ltd,
Bury St Edmunds, Suffolk
Printed and bound in Great Britain by
Mackays of Chatham

www.simonsays.co.uk
www.diannehofmeyr.com

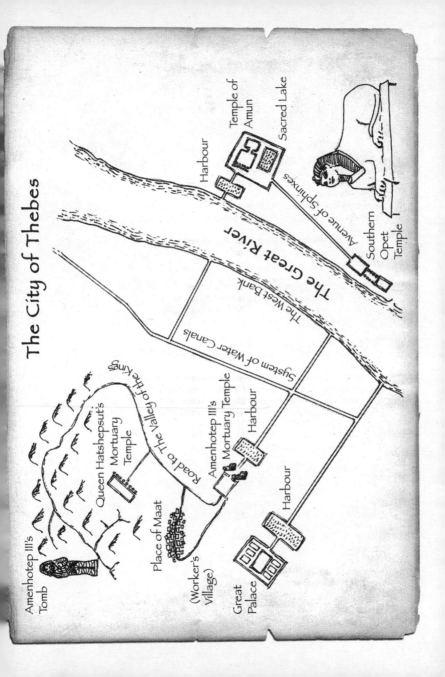

The City of Thebes

Amenhotep III's Tomb

Queen Hatshepsut's Mortuary Temple

Place of Maat

The Valley of the Kings

Road to

(Worker's Village)

Amenhotep III's Mortuary Temple

Great Palace

Harbour

Harbour

System of Water Canals

The West Bank

The Great River

Harbour

Temple of Amun

Sacred Lake

Avenue of Sphinxes

Southern Opet Temple

PROLOGUE

He has a sense of foreboding. As if at any moment something will loom up out of the shadows next to him. The darkness and the sounds of the night, the rustlings, squeaks and sighs that sough through the air have set his imagination running. An owl swoops down. The sharp cry of its prey ends in a strangled screech. An uneasy silence follows. He feels the skin on his arms prickle and his heart quicken.

Who's there? He wants to call out. But there is nothing except the hoarse bark of a dog coming from a distance and the sharp, dry smell of dust and a more pungent smell that pinches his nose. Perhaps a desert fox, prowling for scraps of food at the offering altars.

He glances about uneasily, his eyes running slowly over his surroundings.

The towering statue of his father glares down from

his pedestal, the stony eyes narrowed and unblinking, the edges of his gigantic nostrils flaring, the carved line of his lips sneering. Behind the statue, the Temple of Amun is silent and secretive, its pillars and stones sliced into blocks of light and shade by the bloodless moon. Creatures etched into the stone walls – curved claws, jagged snouts, fierce fangs – are frozen into silence. And throats and chests of enemies are forever stilled as they wait for the arrows directed at their hearts.

His fingers rest on the sculpture of the giant scarab beetle polished with the touch of so many hands. He feels the uneven paving stones still warm under his feet and the crunch of stones beneath his sandals. He has been away a long time. It's strange to be back. After the emptiness of the desert with its distant horizon and the wide, monotonous stretches of river, his eyes are no longer used to the limits set by the stone walls and mud dwellings that anchor Thebes to the Great River.

Here, beside the moon-splintered lake, he feels trapped. This is the wrong place to have agreed to meet his brother. The Inner Sanctum might have been safer. In the Inner Sanctum the spirit of the gods would surely protect the son of a king against the dark evils of the night. But no one knows he has returned to Thebes. He has made sure to keep his identity secret. At all costs he has to speak to his brother first. He needs his protection.

Perhaps it's foolish to have come. Something is wrong. But already it is too late.

A sense of something behind him, an imperceptible movement, makes him turn. He sees the half-expected shadow. The face made pale by the moonlight. The hand clutching an object that glints.

In the moonlight the dagger is sharp and hard and unforgiving.

'You!' The sound escapes his throat more like a cry for help than a word of recognition.

The blade finds the soft spot just below his ribs and angles upward, seeking his heart. Two quick thrusts. Hard and brutal. The blows make him gasp with their suddenness. No words are possible now. He feels the sharp burn of the blade as the dagger is swiftly withdrawn.

The hand that clutches the hilt, he knows well. It's unmistakable. When he wrenches his eyes away and looks down at his chest he sees the huge, black stain seeping through his tunic. Too large and surely too dark to be his blood. He slams his fist against his chest. Presses harshly with both hands at the place. As if in pushing down he will stop his life-blood from flowing from his body. But even as he does it he knows it's too late.

He looks straight up into the eyes opposite him and sees the same answer in them.

Someone calls his brother's name. Over and over. A voice that's surely not his own. It threads and weaves through the darkness.

Around him the night pants like a savage creature. The sky expands. The stars reel. A heartbeat thrums in his ears, louder and louder, until he hears nothing but the sound exploding inside him.

PART ONE

CHAPTER ONE

THE MARKET

Thebes is the colour of chalk. A mixture of sand swirling up from the desert and dust billowing down from the ancient limestone mountains. It sifts down over the city like the finest of bread flours. And this morning, hordes of people with handcarts and donkeys pushing their way through the narrow streets kicked up enough dust to choke us all.

Despite this, a shiver of anticipation ran through me. It was rumoured this would be the best market ever. Traders had arrived from far-off Syria, bringing with them exotic oils, woven cloths, spices and nuggets of precious desert stone said to be as large as duck eggs. Could there be *anything* as exciting as a foreign market?

But the morning had started off badly. On the west bank there'd been no ferryman to take us across the Great River. Crowds had grown with children squalling and mothers scolding, as people from the workers' village gathered. When a boat finally came, the crush was so great that an old woman had fallen from the quayside and disappeared under the water.

'Oi! She's not coming up! Quickly, do something!'

'A crocodile's got her!'

'If a crocodile's got her, *you* won't be coming back either,' someone warned a boy who stood teetering on the edge of the ferry, ready to jump in after her.

He dived in all the same and came up dragging the gasping woman. They were hauled back onto the ferry and people laughed and teased the old woman as they picked off strands of waterweed from her hair and dripping tunic.

All this had taken time. Eventually when we got to the east bank, I was carried along by a surge of people like debris being swept down by a great flood. Men, women, large and small, old and young, all mingled with loud shrieks and yelps ringing out as carts were overturned, or a child fell to the ground, or a dog was trodden underfoot. And in the midst of this some geese had escaped their cage and were honking and hissing and snapping at passing feet.

A pestilence of flies! And now my tunic hem was dragging in the dirt and through some fresh donkey droppings as well.

There was a loud curse behind me. 'Oi! Mind where you're going, stupid girl!'

I barely had time to save myself from falling under the wheels of a woman's handcart piled high with onions and leeks, when someone held out a hand to steady me.

'Watch out! They'll flatten you as quickly as oxen trampling through a barley field,' he shouted above the noise of the honking geese. 'Here, come to the side of the road. You're limping.'

I glanced at the boy as he bent to examine my foot. He looked familiar.

'Your sandals are ridiculous, with their upturned tips! No wonder you tripped! You should be wearing strong leather sandals on market day!' He pressed around my ankle.

'Ouch! That hurt!' I snapped at him.

'It's only twisted. But it needs to be bound.'

I pulled away and tried to stand. 'I'm fine, thank you!'

'You're not! Sit down again. I'll bind it for you.'

I looked back at him. A handsome boy. Long, dark eyelashes. Smooth, freshly-shaven cheeks. No formal wig. His hair falling in damp tendrils against his neck. 'Aren't you the boy who saved the old woman?'

He caught my glance and shrugged. 'Saving old ladies or princesses, it's all the same to me!'

'Princesses?'

He raised a dark eyebrow and grinned at me. 'Your rough cloak doesn't fool me. I can see by the fine linen of your tunic that you're no country girl come into town on market day. You don't belong here, do you?'

I glanced quickly over my shoulder in case anyone had overheard.

'Don't look so dismayed. Your secret won't be told. It's safe with me.'

'I'm . . .' But he'd taken my words away. I brushed his hand from my foot and stood up quickly. He jumped up just as abruptly and pulled me against his chest.

'What . . .?' I gave him a sharp shove with my elbow. 'What do you think you're doing? Let go of me!'

'I will, as soon as that donkey has passed. You almost got yourself knocked down again. Now sit calmly while I bandage your foot.' Then he grinned up at me. 'I know what I'm doing. This isn't the first time I've done this. Trust me.'

He drew a dagger from his girdle, stuck its point

into the linen of his tunic and deftly tore a strip from the hem. Then he began winding the strip firmly under my foot and around my ankle. I eyed him as he worked. His hands were quick and seemed practised at bandaging. His forearms were criss-crossed with hieroglyphs of pale scars and the fingers of his right hand looked as if they'd once been badly broken. I guessed he was about the age my brother would have been. About sixteen or seventeen.

He glanced up and caught me examining him. I felt my face grow hot. He smiled back at me with perfect, even teeth. He was truly handsome.

'You're not from Thebes, are you?'

'How do you know?'

'The stupid upturned sandals. The braided style of your wig. Are you Syrian? Perhaps from Tyre, or Byblos, or even Kadesh?'

I shook my head.

'You're not Nubian.'

I shook my head again.

'From where, then?'

'You ask too many questions.'

He laughed and released my foot and stood up quickly. 'There. The way is clear now.' He bowed slightly, as if giving me permission to leave.

'Clear?' I turned to look at the people brushing past

11

us, wishing another trail of donkeys could delay me. 'I'm from Mitanni. The people here call it Naharin. But I prefer its proper name.'

'Naharin? That far? So you *are* a princess! A princess sent from Naharin to Thebes as a gift to the King.'

'I'm *not* a princess!'

'But you *are* from the Palace?'

I glanced sharply at him. 'What makes you say that?'

'Why else are you wearing a peasant's wrap over a fine linen tunic? You've sneaked out and you don't want anyone to recognise you. But mysterious girls with cats tattooed on their shoulders are easy to recognise.'

'Cats?' I'd forgotten the tattoo of the cat on my shoulder and snatched at my cloak so that it covered the mark. A blush crept up my neck. He was smiling. This boy was a flirt. Yet even though I knew he was flirting, I was still charmed.

'I have to hurry,' I said quickly.

'Go then, Little Cat Girl.'

'That's not my proper name.'

He smiled and held my eyes with his direct look. 'To name something is to know it. But beware of carts and donkeys!'

12

And boys with dark, flirting eyes, I almost threw back at him. But he turned before I could say anything and slipped into the crowd and disappeared.

My sandals were nowhere to be seen. Standing barefoot in the dust, I really *did* feel like a proper country girl. A pestilence of flies! I'd have to walk barefoot through the muck and my ankle would slow me down. The sun was stinging hot. And now I was late. And Kiya would be impatient for her perfect length of cloth.

'Fine linen, woven with gold thread, with tasselled edges and a pattern of turquoise beads caught into it.'

'How can you be sure I'll find such a cloth?'

'The traders are from Syria. Everything at the market will be wonderful.' She had sighed heavily. 'I wish I could go with you.'

'But you can't and that's that! It's too dangerous.'

'Please, Ta-Miu,' she had begged.

But all her flouncing and flopping about on her bed hadn't convinced me. I couldn't risk it. Kiya was too impulsive. She'd draw attention to us.

'I promise to behave.'

But when she saw nothing would make me change my mind, she pouted and said, 'Bring woollen cloth as well.'

'*Wool?* This isn't the Khabur Mountains, Kiya. We don't need wool here.'

'It's not the cloth I need! But the comfort of it. I miss the feel of it beneath my fingers. Four years in Thebes hasn't cured me of longing for things that remind me of home.'

I sighed. Sometimes Kiya – Princess Tadukhepa to others, but always Kiya to me – still seemed such a child. How would she ever cope with her position as wife to the new king?

By the time I eventually reached the market, it was seething with people. Over the stench of donkey droppings came aromas of sizzling goat meat and perfumed wafts of cinnamon, caraway, coriander, saffron, mint, thyme and every other conceivable herb and spice. Hawks whirled overhead trying to snap up entrails and were shooed off by angry stall-holders. Their screeches added confusion to the sound of foreign tongues, donkeys braying, voices arguing over goods and volleys of slaps and curses coming from every direction as tempers flew and the day grew more and more stifling.

I strained to see through the crowds and kept a lookout for the boy. In the noise and riff-raff of people pushing me this way and that, it was all I could do to edge my way forward, cursing myself for not even asking his name. He had come close to guessing mine. Little Cat Girl, he'd called me. But in a city as large as Thebes I'd probably never lay eyes on him again. And who was to say he was even Theban? He might merely be passing through for the market and by tomorrow be gone and on his way to another place.

Eventually I came to a stall piled high with woven fabric and trimmings. I rifled through them and when I saw a cloth I thought would make Kiya happy, bargained as hard as I could, shrugging off others who tried to grasp it from me. Eventually a small sachet of ten carnelians tipped into the trader's hand did the trick. With the cloth firmly bundled under my arm, I shouldered my way through the crowds and came to a space where I could right my clothing and breathe freely again.

The cloth was woven with a pattern of fine red thread and hung with tassels but had no beads of turquoise or gold. Not exactly what Kiya had described but no matter. Perhaps I could sew on some beads. I knew what was behind her wanting something unusual and exotic for the banquet. At this first proper gathering of all the Royal Wives since Nefertiti's marriage to Amenhotep the Younger, Kiya,

15

being the very youngest of all his wives, needed to make an impression.

Suddenly someone grabbed me around the waist and held a hand over my mouth. I felt hot breath at my ear and a whisper. 'It's only me!' He released me slowly and as I spun around I found myself looking straight into the dark-haired boy's eyes.

'Are you following me?' I snapped.

'Only for your protection.'

'Well, *don't*! I don't need your protection! I've travelled across the deserts of Syria on my own.'

He smiled knowingly. 'Not entirely on your own. Weren't you accompanied by hordes of fierce horsemen as protectors?'

I looked over my shoulder. 'Keep your voice down!' I urged.

'In this hubbub no one will hear us. Here, these are yours.' He held up my sandals with a smile that seemed to mock the upturned toe. 'I found them alongside the road. Come. I know a place where we can get something to drink.' He gripped my arm and guided me firmly down a tangle of narrow streets to a small alleyway where there were fewer people. At the bottom of the narrow space I could see a glint of green as the river flowed by. An old man was sitting in a dark doorway. The boy handed him a bag of dates. In return the man poured out two horn cupfuls of pomegranate juice and pushed two honey cakes towards us.

The juice was slightly bitter but cool. I hadn't realised how thirsty I was. The boy drank quickly which left him with a pink moustache. It was difficult not to smile. 'I can't stay long. Tadukhepa is waiting.'

'Tadukhepa?'

'Princess Tadukhepa . . . my mistress.' I wiped the crumbs of honey cake from my lips. 'Although she's really three years younger than I.'

'The *real* princess!' His eyes glinted in the shadowy light. 'So I was right! You travelled from Naharin with a princess. You *did* have fierce horsemen as your protectors, the finest and most valiant of horsemen, famous for the way they train horses. Even the Hittites are jealous of them. And now you live at the Palace here in Thebes.'

'Are you asking or telling?'

'You don't have to be secretive. I can keep secrets.'

'Perhaps another time. I must hurry now.'

'Meet me again. Here tomorrow at the same time?'

Hmm? No *please* or *will you* from this boy. But I liked his charm. I shrugged. 'Perhaps.'

'Perhaps is good enough! Hurry then, before you're missed. You've a banquet to attend.'

I gave him a sharp glance. 'How do you know?'

He smiled. 'In Thebes, it's not only dust that fills the air.'

I took the less crowded route back to the river. Next to the new Southern Opet Temple a smell of myrrh drifted out into the air. In the sunlight that slanted through the columns into the forecourt, I caught sight of priests making offerings before the altars. As they swung their censers, their mumbled intonations echoed against the shining blocks of stone and the newly-carved, tall papyrus-shaped columns. With the Temple so recently built, I knew they needed to make sure the gods were happy and would keep the harmony and order of the world.

Apart from the priests, there was no one else in sight. Not even the urchin boys who usually hung about pelting each other with pebbles and pestering people for a loaf or two of bread. Or even the temple-cleaning women.

I hurried as quickly as my ankle would allow down the avenue of sphinxes guarding the east and the west horizons that led from the Southern Opet Temple to the Temple of Amun. Along the way, I stopped to touch the seventeenth lioness facing east, the one I always touched, with the strange expression that made her look wiser than the rest. Her body was warm under my hand. So much power trapped in her stone-lion muscles.

Then I hurried along through the dark bands of shadow cast by their bodies across the paved avenue. As I passed from shadow to sunlight, it felt as if I was zithering over the strings of a giant lyre. I seemed to catch some inaudible vibration floating upwards. My feet were light as air. My heart sang.

CHAPTER TWO

THE HEART SCARAB

A sound of angry voices and a scrape of footsteps approaching on the gravel of the courtyard made me pause in the middle of undoing the bandage around my ankle. The voices were coming from behind some pillars on the other side of a colonnade.

'It has to be done!' a girl's voice hissed.

'It's too soon!' a man answered back.

'It's never too soon. I *must* be obeyed.'

'But this is not the way. You'll only alienate them.'

'I *must* have rules.'

'There's no point in making rules only for the purpose of making them.'

'Rules give me power. Control. Besides, I can't have them flaunting themselves before Amenhotep.'

Amenhotep? King Amenhotep, the Younger? Was it *Nefertiti* speaking? But who was she talking to?

I held myself very quiet in my hiding place that was not really a true hiding place at all. If they'd chosen to walk this way, I'd immediately have been spotted next to the rill of water where I'd been about to bathe my foot. But there was nothing to be done now except sit still and listen.

'Did you learn *nothing* from his mother, Queen Tiy? She was able to charm people to do as she wished *without* laying down laws that would alienate them.'

'I'm *not* his mother.'

'But your youth and beauty will draw people to your side. You don't have to fight for attention. Take heed of how Queen Tiy governed. She was a woman of great passion, just like you. She achieved much in her lifetime and had an entire Palace at her bidding, her own perfumery, a Royal Barge, a lake built for her pleasure and her own Temple erected as far away as Abu Island on the edge of Nubia.'

'Tchh! Queen Tiy this! Queen Tiy that! I'm sick of her name!'

'But she earned respect and at the same time made sure all her husband's other wives were secondary.'

'It's your fault, Wosret.'

I held myself rigid. So it was Wosret, the Highest of High Priests, whom Nefertiti was talking to.

'Why did you recommend my husband take on his father's wives? It could all have ended,' I heard Nefertiti snap her fingers, 'just like that, if you'd changed the rule. I could've been his first and *only* wife.'

'I couldn't. Tradition must be upheld. Kings of Egypt have always had many wives. What would it imply to their enemies if they didn't? Your father-in-law, King Amenhotep, was the most powerful man in the world. He had one great advantage. Not just military might, but *gold*. Even the greatest of foreign kings were desperate for Egypt's gold and were prepared to beg for it. The King gave them gold but always left them wanting more. They exchanged gifts, not blows. In return for the gold, they gave him the most precious gift of all . . . a foreign princess as a wife, plus her dowry and attendants. King Amenhotep employed personal ambassadors to find him the very best brides. The Palace was full of the most beautiful daughters of the most powerful kings. It was about brotherhood between the great kings.'

'I know all this! And I don't *care*. Now I have to contend with that young, pretty one from Naharin . . . Princess Tadukhepa.'

Tadukhepa? I sat as still as I could. What would Nefertiti say about Kiya?

'Princess Tadukhepa is not a rival. She's a child still. And as Queen, you *must* care about what people think of your husband. I bestowed his father's wives on him to show his power, not only to the foreign kings but to the people of Egypt as well. What would they think if their new king only had *one* wife?'

'It's none of their business,' Nefertiti answered crisply.

'Yes, but it's entirely mine. I want you to be supreme. But you're headstrong. I'm here to guide you. Trust me. If the Palace wives want to enjoy little diversions of luxury, what does it matter? Let them get on with it. Let them play their silly games of dressing up. You are superior.'

'Don't *lecture* me, Wosret!' Nefertiti snapped back.

'I do it for your own good. Fourteen is very young to be ruling a country as powerful as Egypt. *Someone* must guide you.'

'I don't need guidance. I'm the First Royal Wife. And the First Royal Wife must be listened to and obeyed.'

So it *was* her. I craned my neck to get a better view. Yes, it was *definitely* Nefertiti standing there against the sunlight. Even though she wore no crown or royal headdress, I could tell by her distinctive long neck and the way she held her head. And the man, with his clean-shaven head, was definitely the Highest of High Priests, Wosret. Who else would have the courage to tell Nefertiti what she could or could not do?

'And if you're wise, you'll make sure you give him a child soon.'

'What? Never!'

I could hear the shock in her voice.

'All you have to do is produce a boy prince and you'll be the darling of all Egypt.'

'How can you even think I'd want a baby? I'm far too young. I don't want my stomach swollen, or the sickness that comes with it, or *anything* to do with babies!' I heard her stamp her foot. 'You lied to me, Wosret. You said I must marry Amenhotep. You didn't say anything about having children. I'm not going to walk around like an ox while that slip of a Naharin princess flits about like a dragonfly.'

'You don't have to compete. Your beauty is beyond any in the land.'

'What if the child's a girl?'

'It won't be a girl. But if it is, you must have another, until a boy is born.'

'*Enough!* I'm not listening any more.'

The priest sighed heavily. 'The advice is for your

own good. We are kindred spirits in Thebes. We want the same. Your name must be written up in stone. I want you to be the most brilliant and powerful queen Egypt has ever known.'

'It will be so!'

'Then listen to me, Nefertiti. Tread carefully. *Mould* people to your wishes. Don't be in such a hurry. Stealth is required. Believe me, I know! A soft paw treads better than one with claws unsheathed. Have patience. Your husband, Amenhotep, is young. You must guide him. As Queen there are facts you must be familiar with. You must know of territorial disputes, of cattle and herd numbers, of reservoirs and food supply, of records of rainfall and varying levels of the Great River during its flood.'

'What? I'm a *queen*, not a farmer! My Chief Vizier can look after those matters.'

'Yes, but documents need your seal to be authentic and binding. Tax records, storehouse receipts, crop assessments and agricultural statistics, all need your seal. You're supposed to read the reports.'

'That's too boring! You *can't* expect me to read them!'

'*You* won't have to. *I'll* read them. I'll be your advisor. You'll only have to make your seal. Trust me! Family members, particularly those who hold a claim to the throne, can *never* be trusted. I'll be your guide.'

What? *Trust* Wosret? Never! I knew him too well. Without meaning to, I jumped up. There was a small tinkling sound at my feet. A piece of glass lay on the stone step. It could only have fallen from the bandage.

Wosret's voice broke off. 'What was that?'

I stood still as a stone pillar.

'Who knows? It could've been a myriad of things. A cricket chirping. The water in a rill. A servant dropping something.'

'Our discussions are secret. They mustn't be overheard. Come, it's getting late and nearly time for the banquet. I urge you, Nefertiti, take my advice . . .' His voice trailed off as they moved away and disappeared down the colonnade, their sandals making a crunching sound as they walked.

Only when they'd gone did I dare pick up the piece of glass. I sat with my feet dangling in the rill of water and held it in the palm of my hand. It caught the light of the setting sun and glinted back at me. A scarab beetle. Symbol of the god, Khepera. The Creator God who rolled the sun across the sky. The kind of amulet that was layered into a mummy's bandages to act as a source of life that would ignite the real heart in the Afterlife.

There was a hole between the scarab's front feelers

so it could be worn as a charm. Its body was of plain blue glass, but the wings had been made with inlaid slices of coloured green and purple glass that mirrored the lustre on a real scarab.

I rubbed my thumb across it and stared out through the courtyard and felt the feathery tickle of tiny fish swimming past my feet in the rill. The air was flinty with the smell of hot wet stone. In the west, the tall cypress trees stood like dark statues against a sky the colour of pomegranate juice. The last red gash of sunset shone through the dip in the mountains of the desert – the Gap of Abydos.

How had the scarab got between the wraps of bandage on my foot? There was only one person who could have put it there. But why?

Everything was happening too quickly for me to catch up with my thoughts.

CHAPTER THREE

KIYA'S QUARTERS

Kiya was waiting for me in her chambers, sitting in the middle of her bed with clothes strewn about her, earnestly watching her pet chameleon crawl along her hand towards a dead fly balanced on her forearm. Lined up on the bed was a collection of more dead flies and beetles.

She jumped up as she saw me and sent the insects scattering. 'I thought you'd never come!'

'Be careful, Kiya.' I guided the chameleon from her hand onto a branch inside a special wicker cage.

She grabbed me by the shoulders. 'Where have you been, Ta-Miu? I've been waiting and waiting. Why are your cheeks so pink?'

It was hard to keep things secret from Kiya. I'd

planned to make her drag the news from me but now I was with her, the words tripped off my tongue. 'An old woman fell into the river and had to be pulled out. I injured my foot. A boy helped me. And I overheard an interesting conversation in the Palace courtyard.'

'But what about the market? What was it like? Did you find the cloth? And the people? Were there lots of people?'

'Hundreds.' I tossed my head and laughed at her eagerness. 'Maybe even thousands!'

'And acrobats and fire-eaters?'

I nodded. 'And talking monkeys too!'

'Talking monkeys?'

'I'm just teasing. There weren't really talking monkeys!'

Kiya sighed heavily as she sank back on her rumpled bed and flicked the insects away with quick, angry movements. 'I knew I should've gone with you. I could've been disguised as well.'

'My disguise wasn't enough.'

'What?' Her eyebrows shot upwards. 'You mean you were noticed?'

'Not exactly.'

'What then?'

'I met someone.'

Kiya swivelled around to face me. 'Who?'

29

'A boy. Or rather, a young man.'

'A boy? The one who helped you? So *that's* why your cheeks are pink! Who is he?'

'I don't know his name.'

'What was he like? Egyptian or foreign?'

I shook the cloth so its ends floated up into the air to distract her. 'Look what I bought.'

She grabbed hold of it and lifted the gossamer-fine length up against the lamplight and ruffled the threaded tassels. 'Perfect! Nefertiti will wish *she* had been at the market.'

I held out the glass scarab. 'And I found this.'

'Found it?'

I shrugged. 'The boy gave it to me.'

'The mysterious boy!' Her eyes sparkled with excitement. 'What a fine gift. He must be in love.'

'Stop teasing! I hardly know him.'

Kiya cradled the scarab in her hands and drew the lamp nearer. 'It must have cost him dearly. Look closely. It's no ordinary glass scarab. Look at the brilliance on the wings. He must be *very* rich. Perhaps he's a foreign prince come to find an Egyptian bride.'

'Foreign princes don't search for their own brides. And he didn't really give it to me. I found it between the bindings he wound around my foot. I'm not sure he meant me to have it.'

'Of course he did, Ta-Miu. He was just too shy to give it to you directly.' She untied a thick rope of twisted gold from around her neck, threaded the scarab on it and retied it around my neck. 'You must perform the sacred ritual to bring out its magical power. That way you will be truly blessed whenever you wear it. Is he handsome?'

'Perhaps.'

She gave me a quick look. 'More handsome than Tuthmosis?'

'I can't say.' The glass scarab lay cool against my skin alongside the ankh key Tuthmosis had given me the night he'd left Thebes, when I'd arranged a boat for his escape. I'd not laid eyes on him since. It was rumoured he'd been captured by a tribe of fierce Medjay, somewhere in the desert.

Kiya laughed. 'The serving girls were all in love with him. Remember how they tagged behind him and made flower wreaths and dared each other to put one across his shoulders, giggling behind their hands every time he turned and gave them disparaging looks.'

I thought of Tuthmosis with his dark lashes and strange blue eyes and how he'd beguiled us both when we first arrived at the Palace. We'd scarcely looked at the younger brother, Amenhotep, who'd been too busy making model reed boats and floating them in the canals. Tuthmosis was broad-shouldered. Good with a bow. And, despite his leg injury, stealthy at bringing down waterfowl with his throwstick. The hooded falcon he carried on his wrist had made him even more alluring. We'd followed him about as starry-eyed as the serving girls.

I shrugged. 'They had no claim on him. It was *you*, Kiya, who was to be his wife.'

'And now? Where do you think Tuthmosis is now?'

'I wish we knew.' In the small silence that followed we both listened to the clear liquid notes of Kiya's pet Golden Oriole as it sang from its cage next to her bed.

Suddenly Kiya shivered as if touched by a feather. 'I can't bear the thought of him a prisoner in a Medjay camp in the deserts of Nubia. And now, I'm betrothed to his brother, Amenhotep the Younger.' She gave a deep sigh.

I glanced across at her. By the light of the oil lamps, her face, with its slightly upturned nose, looked very young and innocent. 'Amenhotep will treat you kindly. And I'll be here with you.'

'It's not Amenhotep I worry about, it's Nefertiti.'

I shook my head. 'It's *Wosret* you should worry about. Wosret planned to kill Tuthmosis. When something is in Wosret's way, he gets rid of it. He can't be trusted. Not *ever*!'

I glanced at the serving girls who were carrying urns of water and preparing the oils and unguents for Kiya's bath, and dropped my voice. 'Listen to what I heard Wosret say to Nefertiti tonight . . .'

While I sprinkled the new cloth I'd bought with rose water to get rid of the smell of the trader's rags and chase off any stray fleas, I told Kiya what I'd overheard in the courtyard.

An attendant stood fidgeting next to Kiya. 'You're going to be late, Princess Tadukhepa. We need to pin and arrange your wig now.'

Kiya pulled a small face and took up a bronze mirror from the table on which her ivory combs and brushes and glass phials of perfumes stood. Two girls began to arrange the braids of her wig. She glanced at me in the mirror, the golden lamplight flickering over her earnest expression. 'What do you suppose they were secretly planning?'

I shrugged. 'Wosret never *plans*. He only *plots*! Tonight we must be vigilant.'

'Let's hurry, then!' She swung around to face me. 'You must help me, Ta-Miu. Tonight I must dazzle everyone and show them that a princess from Mitanni can stand up to an Egyptian queen. I'll wear the cloth

33

you bought tied in place around my waist with an emerald brooch and wear my largest gold disc earrings as well.'

I laughed. 'You'll spark life into the night like a jewel.'

Kiya wrinkled her nose. 'It's hard to be a jewel when Nefertiti herself is so flawless.'

'Be brave now! You forget she's half Mitannian, even though she claims to be entirely Egyptian now that she's the First Royal Wife.'

'Maybe that's why she dislikes me so much.'

CHAPTER FOUR

THE PRISON – TA-MIU

The boy has charm. It was his charm that led me astray. Now here I am in prison, and not even Kiya speaking up for me has saved me from Nefertiti's decision.

Charm is a strange word. It can be a trinket or object worn to ward off evil as well as the spell that protects or even brings about evil to the person it's used against. But it is also something less tangible. It's the power to give delight. An enticing quality that causes fascination.

The boy did both. He gave me a charm. But he also charmed and fascinated me.

Kiya said I must perform the sacred ritual to bring out the magic of the glass scarab he gave me. I knew the ritual. Place the amulet on a table on top of a piece of olive wood with a pure linen cloth below. Put censers of myrrh in the middle of the table and a jar of chrysolite into which you've mixed an ointment of lilies and cinnamon. Take the amulet and lay it in the ointment. Leave it for three days. Then remove it and anoint yourself with the mixture early in the morning and recite the prayer of the scarab. Afterwards make a sacrifice of fresh bread and seasonal fruits threaded on vine sticks.

But it was false. I did all this. Yet the scarab *hadn't* protected me.

'Scratch, scratch, scratch! That's all you do. What are you scratching at? No amount of scratching on these walls will get you out. Are you listening to me? I'm your neighbour. I'm here in the cell next door. What is it you're doing?'

'Writing.'

'What?'

'Words.'

'But what words? Are you a scribe? Are you making lists?'

'No.'

'Then what do you write, if not lists? What words?'

'Words that will help me understand.'

'Understanding doesn't come from *words*. Understanding is in the *head*. So you might as well stop your writing now.'

I threw down the ankh key. It was just my luck to have a talkative neighbour!

I paced out the steps. The cell was exactly six paces by five and, by the looks of the scum lines on the thick, mud-brick walls, had once been flooded.

'*Now* what are you doing?'

'Walking.'

'Walking won't get you out. They've done it before, you know. Backwards and forwards. Pacing is useless. No amount of pacing has ever got anyone out. Just wears out your sandals on the stone.'

I scratched at the paving stones with my bare hands. Every tile was fixed. And the walls were solid. The only light came in through a narrow slit at ceiling height. Too narrow for even the smallest shoulders to squeeze through. I pulled the bed pallet across and rolled it up to give extra height.

'*Now* what is it that you're doing?'

'Looking out.'

'Hah! I know. You're standing on the bed pallet. I've done that too. But I've given up. All you see are feet passing at ground level. Ugly they are.'

'What?'

'The feet. Never see any refined feet. It's all calluses and veins and filthy uncut toenails that pass by here. Feet with mud between the toes, so it looks as if they've walked through a cow byre. This is a poor part of town. There are no jewelled toes or anklet bracelets to be seen in these parts.'

I stood on tiptoes and had a glimpse of glinting water between clumps of reed and papyrus and the view of the prow of a boat sliding past. A distant *shrr shrr* sound of sistrums and chanting voices told me I was near one of the temples.

'Do you hear that? The sistrums and the chanting? On and on. It never stops. Could drive an old woman mad. But I've become used to it.'

The cell was hot and stank of urine and more besides and there were flies everywhere. I shooed as many as I could out of the narrow slit opening and tore a strip off my tunic and tied it over the bars to prevent more from entering.

'What do you look like?' came the insistent voice from next door. 'I wish I could see you. But even if I squeeze my head against my cell gate, I can't catch a glimpse of you. Your voice sounds young.'

I sighed as I picked up the ankh again. 'I *am* young.'

'Are you writing again?'

I ignored her. It was more than just sistrums and

chanting that could drive a person mad. *She* was driving me mad. Making my thoughts churn with her chattering. I threw down the ankh again and flung myself down on the pallet, but jumped up soon enough. It felt as if my body had been rubbed with burning chillies. I was itching all over and covered in red bumps. It came from more than just palm fibres that stuck through the woven covering of the pallet.

'Hah! I can hear they've got you! You'll get used to them. Eventually you don't even bother to scratch. Just let them crawl and bite.'

How long would I have to endure this? This filthy place, where the only washing facility was a stone trough of dirty water and a gutter that sloped towards a stinking hole in the floor? Even the lowliest of servants in the Palace had better toilet facilities. And it was no good shouting or shaking the barred gate. I had tried both and was given abuse by the guards that sat beyond where I could see.

'No good putting up a fuss, deary,' the woman had called out. 'They're going to take no notice of you. Unless they feel like having a bit of frolic. Doesn't do any good to show you're feisty. It's the feisty girls they love. Makes the conquest seem even better. So don't fuss them. Just shut your mouth and take what you get.'

'It's *unjust*! I haven't committed any crime! I can prove it.'

'That's what they *all* say, them that come in here! And those down the corridor don't care whether you're guilty or not! I should know. Been here long enough now!'

'How long?' I jabbed the ankh at the mud brick.

'Can't say exactly. I scratch marks on the walls. Take note of the festivals. I think I've seen seven Opet festivals go by.'

'*Seven*! You've been in this place for *seven* years?'

'Maybe more, deary! Who knows?'

'What did you do to be put in prison for so long?'

'Stole some bread.'

'Bread? You've been here for *seven* years for stealing bread?'

'I think they've forgotten me. I've no family to plead my cause.'

'Praise Horus! Don't let them forget me too! Samut will come for me.'

'Ah, Samut! And would that be your young man? Don't depend on it. Young men find new girlfriends that cause less trouble.'

I leant my forehead against the cool, mud-brick wall. But I hadn't caused trouble. I was not to blame.

I *had* to speak to Samut. My last words to Kiya were: 'Tell Samut they've taken me.'

'Not speaking now. Sulking are you? Why are you here, then?'

I wouldn't answer.

'Don't tell, then. I'll use my imagination. Let's see . . . was it for—'

'They say I stole a ring from King Amenhotep's tomb.'

'*Tomb robbing!* You'll be here for more than *seven* years then, deary!'

'But I didn't! I'm *not* a tomb robber! The ring was given me.'

'Hah! By a tomb robber, no doubt!'

'Samut's no tomb robber!'

'Ah, the boy again! Now you're protecting him. Well, he won't come for you. Believe an old woman's word. He'll be protecting his own skin. You won't see the likes of him here.'

'That's not true. He loves me.' I shook the gate hard. I would've shaken her too if I'd been able to lay my hands on her.

'That's what they all say! No, you'll have to think of someone else to save you!'

I turned away from the gate.

'Now you've gone all silent again. Is it something

41

I said to upset you? Don't stop talking. It's been lonely here. The man who was there before you was a very silent creature. Then he died.'

I held my hands to my ears and flung myself back on the pallet. She was wrong! Samut *would* come! Kiya would make sure. They wouldn't let me stay here for seven *hours* . . . let alone seven *days* . . . or Hathor help me . . . seven *years*!

'Oh well, when you feel like talking, I'll be here. Not going anywhere myself. My old bones will rot here before *I* get out!'

I beat my fists into the pallet and stifled my sobs against the filthy fabric. Sekhmet, fighting lion-spirit of Hathor, save me. Seventeenth lion save me! Claw at my enemies and bring Samut to me riding on your back!

Soon the itching became too much for me. I slipped down onto the floor and lay my burning cheek against the cold stone. High above me I watched a pair of muddy woven sandals walk past and heard the *clip-clop* of donkey hooves. Flies buzzed around my face and the voices of the temple priestesses intoned endlessly while the words hammered in my head. *Samut will come! Samut will come! He will!*

No! Stop this! I was tired. I needed sleep. Tomorrow I would think straight again.

CHAPTER FIVE

PLUMAGE OF THE GODDESS

The evening air brought out heavy perfumes of fig and musk-rose. And dripping trumpets of moonflower with moths circling about them gave off a scent of sweet, pure honey, as Kiya and I set out.

For every step of the way, our feet were guided by lights. Paths were laid with snail shells filled with citron-scented oil around the immense lake built for Queen Tiy. Drifting on the surface of the lake itself were tiny papyrus floats, each burning with oil. It seemed Nut, the Goddess of the Sky, had allowed an entire armful of stars to topple to earth. Yet the dark sky still held myriads more that reflected back another lake of stars.

A shiver of anticipation went through me. What

could be more exciting than a banquet given by a new Queen?

We passed through the gateway of the Great Hall with its whisper of flags on huge cedar posts. Long low tables arranged around three sides of the Great Hall were already laid. Gold goblets and platters of silver and glass caught fire in the light of flares, and piles of grapes, apricots, plums and pomegranates lay glistening like brilliant jewels on bronze trays. To one side a group of blindfolded Syrian slaves played lyres, while at the far end some girls played harps and double flutes.

Attendants hung flower wreaths around our necks and then offered us sweet-smelling unguents from fine alabaster jars. We touched the unguents to our foreheads and wrists and took fragrant wax cones and placed them on their heads as we were joined by more and more Royal Wives trailing servants and pet monkeys and cats on long leads.

Kiya nudged me. 'See . . . I could have brought my chameleon.'

'And have it eaten by a monkey?'

We sat on low stools while serving girls presented platters of steaming fish and trussed fowl and woven trays of rolled durum wheat flavoured with apricots, pine kernels and rose water. And a team of eight men staggered forward with a wooden board hoisted up on their shoulders that held an entire roasted and honey-glazed Oryx gazelle, complete with its long, dark horns.

Attendants went about continually refilling our goblets with wine. And the Royal Sealer of Wine drew our attention to names like *Star of Horus* and *Height of Heaven* and an ancient Chassut that was as dark and thick and red as blood and marked three times good.

'Just a few sips!' I warned Kiya and added some water to hers so that it was more pale pink than red.

'To us!' she cheered and held her goblet up and gave it a chink against mine. 'And these are my favourites,' she sighed as she took up handfuls of honeyed figs and dates stuffed with pistachios.

It was a feast beyond measure. But there was no sign of Nefertiti. As the evening wore on and more and more wine was drunk, the noise and laughter of the royal women increased. And the cats and monkeys added extra confusion as they bounded about, snarling and hissing and chasing each other on their leads that twined around everyone's legs, and snatching at food from passing trays.

Kiya pulled a face. 'What's taking her so long?'

A flurry of music finally announced the Queen.

45

She entered the Great Hall accompanied by a scowling Wosret, in his priestly leopard cloak. And what an entrance she made! A group of Libyan slaves each with two stiff feathers poking up from their short hair bore gigantic fans made of ostrich plumes, while two Nubian slaves each led young cheetahs that snarled as they stalked alongside. Another Nubian led a small giraffe by a red silken cord – its legs so long and spindly, it looked scarcely old enough to have been weaned from its mother. They were in turn followed by a trail of handmaidens and serving girls too numerous to count, until the entire Great Hall echoed with the sound of sandals slapping against stone, and the *chink chink chink* of bracelets and earrings, and the susurration of floor-sweeping robes, and girls' whispers and stifled giggles, mixed here and there with a sharply whispered rebuke from an older handmaiden.

It was an entrance designed to captivate. All eyes were stuck to her and loud whispers rose up.

'I'd forgotten how young our Queen is!'

'She's such a *child*!'

'But with the figure of a woman! What would I give for a waist like that?'

'Child or not, she knows how to make an entrance!'

46

'What jewels! Have you ever seen anything like them?'

'They say she spends like mad!'

'Look at her cheekbones. Sharp enough to fit into the cup of your hand. I'm sure she's not true Egyptian. Some say her mother was a princess from Naharin.'

'Egyptian or not, with those green flecks in her eyes and long neck, she's beautiful!'

Wosret held his hand up for silence, his dark, lizard eyes darting quickly from side to side. Then he led Nefertiti forward and presented her. 'Great First Royal Wife, Nefertiti, may she live, prosper, and be happy forever!'

Everyone answered back 'Great First Royal Wife, Nefertiti, may she live, prosper, and be happy forever!' then fell silent, awed by her presence.

She was wearing the magnificent Vulture Crown of Egypt that proclaimed her the Foremost Lady of Most Royal of Wives. Topped by tall ostrich plumes and gold sun-discs, it made her taller than anyone in the Great Hall. The gold wings of the Vulture Goddess sweeping past her brows and across her cheekbones gleamed with jewels. And hanging from her ears were the golden, striking cobras of the Cobra Goddess, their red ruby eyes flaring in the lamplight: Protector of Pharaohs.

Her hair fell forward in two dark sections on either side of her face, while the back portion hung heavily netted down her back. Across her shoulders was the broadest of gold broad-collars that stretched right from the base of her long neck to the edge of her shoulders and dipped across her breasts. Beneath that, a tunic fell to the floor, so transparent and finely woven that it outlined every curve of her body. She might still have been a young girl but she certainly *did* have the body of a woman.

I saw Wosret give her a dark look as she turned to him with smile and nodded almost playfully. Then she swept an imperious glance around, meeting the eyes of every woman in the front row and, despite being younger than most in the Great Hall, compelling them by the sheer intensity of her gaze to lower their eyes first, refusing to glance to the next person until they did so.

When it was the turn of Kiya, she inclined her head. 'Ah, the child from Naharin is here. Is it not beyond your bedtime?'

I gripped Kiya's hand to keep her from answering impulsively, knowing full well she was only a year younger than Nefertiti.

Kiya, with all the breeding of her royal Mitanni background, managed a smile and bowed low with both her hands stretched forward in obeisance. 'My Queen, you do me great honour to single me out.'

Secretly I was proud of Kiya. A look of slight annoyance crossed Nefertiti's face. Then her eyes swept quickly on, ignoring mine as if to suggest she'd already lost interest. 'Good! It seems everyone is here!' Then she inclined her head slightly towards Wosret. I was close enough to hear her murmur, 'Now you may leave.'

Wosret bowed but stood firm. 'I prefer to stay.'

She smiled at him. 'Stay then, but take a step backward.' Then she passed in front of him so he could no longer see her face or direct her in any manner. I noticed a quick flash of anger pass across his face.

'I, Nefertiti, the embodiment of the Goddess Tefnut who showers Egypt with rain and kindness, welcome all the ladies of my husband's court. Your King, my husband, King Amenhotep the Younger, sends you greetings this evening and hopes you have enjoyed the banquet.'

I marvelled at her composure. She was standing in front of at least five hundred Royal Wives and handmaidens, many of them much older than herself, being scrutinised by all, yet there was no quaver to her voice.

'I wish to announce . . .' As she paused, I noticed her neck stiffen. Maybe it was the weight of the crown or perhaps, after all, she was trying to give herself courage. My eyes met Kiya's. She pulled a little face and then smiled.

'I wish to announce new rules of conduct. They will supersede any others that have gone before in the Palace.'

There was a noticeable intake of breath as everyone leant forward to hear what Nefertiti would say next. The Palace was governed by what Amenhotep's mother, Queen Tiy, had put in place. It was inconceivable that rules would, or even *could*, change. The Palace, up until her death, had run in perfect harmony for thirty years. There was no jealousy between the wives except for an occasional flare-up which was often more due to moon phases than to true jealousies.

Now, to make sure her point was taken, Nefertiti paused and looked around at the women before she continued. I saw Wosret reach out and try to touch her arm, but with a small, hardly perceptible movement, she created a distance between them.

'We need to curb expenses.'

I raised my eyebrows at Kiya. The court of Egypt was wealthier than any foreign power. We knew all about Egypt's gold. It was gold, after all, that had enticed Kiya's father to send her to Egypt.

Nefertiti gestured to her scribe who was sitting cross-legged alongside, writing his record of the proceedings on a scroll of papyrus. He handed her a separate scroll. She began reading:

'The new rules are as follows: One, the height of any headdress worn by ladies of the Palace may be no higher than a cone of wax.'

'What? A cone of wax? But that's ridiculously low,' someone whispered.

'Two, all exotic forms of dress such as tassels and upturned sandals may no longer be worn.'

Kiya gripped my arm and whispered close to my ear. 'This is *not* about cutting costs. This is aimed directly at *us*! It's an insult!'

I squeezed her hand tightly in case she felt the need to speak out. But others must have felt the same. Nefertiti sent a razor-sharp look around the Great Hall to restore quiet, before she continued. 'It's the custom in Egypt that *adopted* wives from foreign lands retain nothing of their former court.'

Kiya shook her head. 'This is ridiculous!'

'Three, silver, lapis lazuli and emerald may no longer be worn.'

'But Egypt has no silver or lapis lazuli of its own!'

51

Kiya whispered fiercely. '*We* brought chests of lapis from Mitanni as part of my dowry!'

'Shh! Kiya! She'll hear!'

'Four, the amount of gold worn must be limited to the weight equivalent of a pomegranate. And finally . . .' Nefertiti paused, '. . . ladies who arrived in court with large retinues will be required to place some of their serving girls into the service of the Palace rather than keep them for their own private need.'

She looked slowly around the Great Hall. 'The only person exempt from the rules will be *me*. In the course of duty, I have to wear apparel suited to a Queen. We will now enjoy the dancing.' And with that she clapped her hands and ordered the musicians to play and the dancers to begin their performance.

'What cheek! How can she?'

All around me, scarcely hidden by the music of the lyres and harps, was a hubbub and buzz of angry voices, sounding like bees that had had honey stolen from their hive. I watched Wosret's face as he approached Nefertiti. I could see the dark flush on his face. This was not what he'd planned.

Kiya's eyes were flaring with anger. 'She wants to put us down as if we're nothing but dirt under her feet. She wants to remind us that Egypt overran the Kingdom of Mitanni. But that was long ago. Since then, there's been peace between our countries.'

'She's playing a game. Even Wosret is annoyed with her. Did you see his scowling face? She's braver than I thought. She managed to anger not just the Royal Wives but the Highest of High Priests as well!' I grabbed Kiya's arm. 'Quick! They're leaving. We must follow to find out what all this is about.'

'You went against my wishes,' Wosret hissed as we hung back so as not to be seen.

Nefertiti gave him a quick glance. 'Wosret, you have such old-fashioned ideas. It's tiresome.' She pulled her tunic out of reach of the cheetahs that were clawing at each other around her feet. Her lips lifted at the corners in a playful smile. 'You don't always behave properly.'

He gave her a sharp glance and lowered his voice. 'What are you referring to?'

Nefertiti raised a perfectly-plucked eyebrow and smiled. 'I know some of your secrets.'

'Secrets? I have none.'

She waved her hand in the air as if batting away a moth and glanced around at her attendants. 'Did you see the way I commanded the women's attention?

How they looked at me? All I did was cast my eye around the room and everyone immediately fell silent.'

Her attendants giggled. Wosret scowled around at them. 'Tcch! Keep silent, you chattering hoopoes. Have you forgotten how to behave in the presence of the Highest of High Priests? I've matters to discuss with the Queen.'

The girls quickly bowed.

'My entrance music didn't have enough flourish. Remind me to reprimand the musicians tomorrow. It should've been more stirring.'

'Nefertiti, concentrate for a moment.' He kicked out at one of the cheetahs. 'And send these impossible animals as well as these chattering hoopoes away so we can talk properly.'

'Only if you promise not to lecture!' She clapped her hands and dismissed the attendants with a sweep of her arm. 'Off you go. Return to my chambers and wait for me.' Then she reached up and took the plumage of the towering Vulture Crown from her head. 'And take this. I can't stand it a moment longer. Its weight has cut a groove into my forehead. I must devise another crown, equally tall, but not as heavy.' She nodded curtly at the Nubian slaves. 'Keep the cheetahs on cushions at my bedside.'

Then she linked her arm through Wosret's and fell into step alongside him.

His eyes darted across at her. 'Will you listen now?'

'I *am* listening but sometimes you're so *serious*. You behave like an elderly uncle, always telling me what I can and cannot do. Tonight has been a celebration! My first appearance before all the Royal Wives. Don't spoil everything by being cross.'

Kiya and I hung back as she grabbed his sleeve and rushed him along. 'Look at the lake. It's as if the stars have fallen from sky to earth. I can see the constellation of the lion and the scorpion in the water.'

'The lion and the scorpion are in you, Nefertiti! You have the fighting spirit of the lioness Sekhmet at her fiercest, and at the same time the cunning and ruthlessness of the Scorpion Goddess Seqet, breathing life into the world but at the same time knowing just when to sting. Unpredictable. One moment exploding with venom; the next, all charm. You'll make an excellent Queen. But you must tame your lion and scorpion spirit. You *must* learn to obey me.'

'Stop scowling and lecturing, Wosret. Let's show Thebes their new Queen, tomorrow. We'll go up and down the Great River on the Royal Barge. I'll stand under the canopy with all my jewels,' she looked sideways at him and laughed, 'and you, the Highest of High Priests, will be at my side with your leopard cloak, and your fierce looks. Who will resist me?'

Wosret shook his head. 'Your husband, Amenhotep the Younger, will stand at your side.'

Kiya caught my look as we stood in the shadows.

CHAPTER SIX

DAZZLING ATEN

Kiya touched my shoulder. 'How do I look? Do you think anyone will recognise me? I'm too afraid to turn my head in case people are staring.'

'No one is staring, Kiya. But you shouldn't have come. It's dangerous for you in the streets of Thebes without protectors.'

She curled her lips in protest. 'Protectors are for princesses. Today I'm *not* a princess. It's exciting. I'm glad I came with you, Ta-Miu. Now I can judge for myself whether this boy is worthy of you. But all the same, I wish I'd gone with you yesterday . . . even if there *weren't* talking monkeys!'

'Now listen, Kiya, if we're stopped and questioned, you must make a run for it before they discover who you really are. I'll distract whoever stops us while you escape.'

She shook her head. 'I won't return to the Palace without you.'

'You *must*. Thebes is full of brigands. Everyone is on the lookout to make themselves rich. If someone knows you're a princess, they'll capture you and keep you locked up while they bargain for a huge reward.'

She wrinkled her nose. 'I'm not at all scared.'

The marketplace was busy. Down every side alleyway traders had stretched canopies over their doorways as protection from the sun and were selling hair trinkets, jars of honeycomb, bowls of cooked lentils flavoured with spices, dried and salted fish and pale delicate-blue duck eggs lying in baskets alongside platters of ground flour for those who had no time to grind their own. Nearby a small group of men sat in the shade of a mimosa tree, patiently waiting their turn with the barber who worked beneath his sign of the razor, hanging from a branch.

'Come buy and eat!' urged a woman selling artichokes flavoured with dill, lemon and garlic and slices of roasted pumpkin as orange and plump as the sun. 'Come and taste what's good.'

'Listen! Listen to me! Come if you're thirsty. Buy

wine and goat's milk. Honey cakes too, sprinkled with poppy seed.'

Kiya took hold of my arm. 'Let's stop and taste the honey cakes. They look delicious. And look,' she pointed down an alleyway, 'they're baking bread.'

'We can't linger, Kiya.' I pulled her away, but even at the fish stalls with their stink of rotten fish, she stopped to gawp at the dead, silvery fish with their open mouths and entrails spilling out, and stood so close to the flashing knives that she was soon covered in fish scales.

'Never seen a dead fish before, miss?' A boy scraping the fish goggle-eyed her. 'Mind the blood, then. Won't do to get your face all freckled with blood!'

I tugged at Kiya's arm. 'You'll get proper freckles too. Pull that cloth over your face before anyone recognises you. You're burning your skin in the hot sun and now you're covered in fish scales as well!'

She laughed and wrinkled her nose at me. 'Good! I'll look like a true peasant.' Then she nudged me. 'Did you see how that boy eyed you?'

'Silly! It was *you* he was looking at, with your glinting halo of fish scales. He fancied you as a fisherman's wife!'

I led her away from the stalls through a confusing

warren of smaller alleyways, hoping I would still remember the one where the boy and I had drunk pomegranate juice. What curiosity was driving me to meet him again? I'd tossed and turned all night making and remaking my decision. And this morning when I'd told Kiya I was going, she sat there in the middle of her large bed with that fierce, stubborn expression I knew so well.

'You can't go alone! You're treating me like a child who can't go anywhere in case I faint at the sight of something strange. You're my maid, not my mother. I'm old enough to make my own decisions. I'm *ordering* you to take me with you.'

There was no persuading her otherwise.

We skirted past some children kicking a ball made of woven reed with dogs yapping at their heels, and eventually found the alleyway I was looking for. The boy was already there, leaning up against a doorway. And suddenly as I saw him again I felt a small flutter like a moth against my ribcage. I was grateful the shadows hid my pink cheeks.

'Stop a moment!' Kiya held me back. 'I want to look at him first and see if he meets my approval.' She nodded. 'Hmm! Truly handsome. Those dark eyes and broad shoulders. I would have flirted with him too.'

'You're too young! And I didn't flirt with him.'

Kiya looked back knowingly. 'Let's find out more about this secretive boy.'

'For the sake of Hathor, don't say too much,' I warned her.

He smiled as we approached, then glanced across at Kiya.

'She's a friend. A fellow serving girl in the service of the Princess Tadukhepa. I thought it safer not to come alone.'

'If your friend can save you from donkeys, then you're much safer.' He bowed towards Kiya. 'I'm pleased to make your acquaintance. If this is the beauty of the serving girls, what must be the beauty of the Princess Tadukhepa herself?'

I noticed Kiya's lips twitch as she bit back her laughter. She held her hand to her mouth when I scowled across at her. As he led the way through the alleyway down to the river, she made signs behind his back, nodding and smiling her approval while I pressed her arm to keep her quiet.

The riverside was busy. Sacks of grain were being offloaded from boats and scribes were sitting cross-legged on the ground calling out numbers as men passed by with heavy sacks on their backs. The river was low and along the edge, boys were cutting papyrus and trussing and loading the tall plumes into baskets on their backs for the paper-makers. With so many plumes sticking up from their shoulders, they looked like papyrus plants themselves. Fishermen were gutting fish nearby and women were cutting water-lilies. A herd boy who had driven some water buffalo down to the water was trying to control their splashing amidst the confusion as people cursed and shooed them away.

The river was a bad choice if we were to go unnoticed. A group of women doing laundry, rubbing linen cloths with reed sap and thrashing them against some rocks, sucked at their teeth and puckered their lips and eyed us as we passed. I felt them taking note of every detail of our faces, but perhaps they were merely curious to see three idle young people walking about freely, while everyone else had work to do.

Kiya turned and pulled a face at them.

I jerked her arm. 'Stop drawing attention to us.'

We stopped in a quieter bend where brilliant kingfishers were flitting about and some green herons were building a nest. The boy stamped down the reeds and thistles so we could sit in comfort. I looked at the water rushing by and thought of the places it had come from, sweeping down through the rocky cataracts of Nubia, carrying with it smooth black pebbles, desert sand and drowned water-lilies, perhaps the body of a goat and sometimes even the body of a man. The water had touched the stone steps of far-off temples in sunshine and by moonlight and had heard the hollow halls echo back its conversation. It had felt the sun's hot kisses and the caress of the wind over its surface like a hand across the skin, and tasted the moon's tears.

I leant down to scoop up a few sips and thought of Tuthmosis. Perhaps somewhere far upstream, his lips had touched this very same water mine were now touching. When I glanced up, I saw the boy watching as if waiting for me to speak. Suddenly I felt confused. Why had I come to meet him when secretly I still held Tuthmosis so close to my heart?

'My name is Samut,' he said as if to break the silence.

A pestilence of flies! I looked at Kiya in dismay. We'd forgotten to choose a name for her. 'Ta . . .' she had already begun but her voice trailed off as I interrupted. 'Kiya . . .' I blurted out and shook my head, urging her not to say her proper name.

Samut nodded at me, 'So you're Kiya . . .' then turned to Kiya, '. . . and you're Ta?'

'No!' we both said in unison.

His eyebrows shot up. 'How can you be confused about your names?'

'We're not confused. She's Kiya.' I pointed at Kiya. 'And I'm Ta-Miu.'

'The cat tattoo, of course!'

I realised the rough peasant tunic had slipped off my shoulder again.

'So Little Cat Girl was nearly right.'

Kiya glanced across at Samut with a glint in her eyes. 'I said to Ta-Miu, you must be very rich.'

I frowned and nudged her.

'Yes, *very* rich . . . or else the scarab must've come from a mummy wrapping!'

'Hush, Kiya!'

She tossed her head and gave me a look. 'I haven't finished. Or was it given to you by a girl as a token of her heart?'

What had got into her? She'd gone mad! Being set free of the Palace for an afternoon had made her delirious.

Clearly Samut thought Kiya amusing and laughed. 'By the truth of the white feather of Maat, the answer is no to all three. I'm not rich, nor a tomb robber, nor a taker of hearts.'

'So what *is* your secret?' Kiya smiled innocently up at him, wrinkling her nose in the sunlight.

64

'I've none. The scarab was made by a friend who works in the glass furnaces in the workers' village at the Place of Maat.'

I looked up sharply. 'On the west bank? If he lives there, he must be a Royal artisan working for the Palace! You *mustn't* tell him about us.'

Samut's dark eyes glinted like sunlight dancing on the water. He shook his head. Then suddenly he sat up straighter. 'Look ... the Royal Barge, *Dazzling Aten*, is coming this way.'

I scrambled up. Nefertiti! I'd forgotten her plan to appear on the Great River. 'Quick, Kiya! This is dangerous! We mustn't be seen!'

'Don't be ridiculous.' He tugged at my arm. 'You've just arrived. Lie low in the grass and even if the barge passes as close as that water-lily, no one will know you are attendants from the Palace. You look like peasant girls. Only I know differently. If the Princess Tadukhepa was on board, *then* you'd have to be careful.'

I squinted at Samut through the sunlight. Why was he mentioning Princess Tadukhepa? Had he guessed about Kiya?

'What do you mean?'

He shrugged. 'If you work for her, she'd know your faces.'

Kiya shook her head. I could see she could barely control her bubbles of laughter. 'Princess Tadukhepa won't be there. Nefertiti would *never* invite her on the Royal Barge. So there's no harm in watching, is there, Ta-Miu?'

I gave her a sharp look. She'd left us no further option but to stay. I put my hand to my forehead to shield the sun from my eyes. The boat stood out in dark silhouette against the sunlight, its tall prow curving sharply out of the glittering water like the neck of some strange creature. Two figures stood under the canopy.

Kiya made a spyhole with her fingers. 'It's Nefertiti with Amenhotep the Younger alongside her.'

The barge slid effortlessly across the water, propelled by about twenty oarsmen rowing in a slow, measured pace so that it seemed to float. And each time the oars came up they showered the air with glinting jewel-drops.

News spread quickly. Crowds of people were gathering along the banks all eager for a view, everyone pushing for a better place and children squealing to be lifted up on their father's shoulders, with old ladies grumbling and digging their elbows in until they managed to make a space for themselves in the front.

The barge never failed to amaze. A ripple of gasps

went through the crowd as it drew nearer and the full detail of the dazzling designs painted across its sides became apparent. The sharp, upturned, gold-embellished prow that ended in the shape of an opening lotus flower, the gold canopy with the huge Eye of Horus painted on each side, the vast wings of the Vulture Goddess, Nekhbet, stretched across the entire red sail from tip to tip and, emblazoned under the protection of each wing, the cartouches of Amenhotep the Younger and Nefertiti.

It was a spectacle not often seen on an ordinary workday afternoon. A golden boat that made Thebes gleam with its beauty.

Amenhotep was wearing the blue gold-studded Khepresh Warrior Crown with the golden cobra rising over his forehead. His shoulders had broadened since I'd last seen him and across his chest he wore a gold pectoral that flashed in the sunlight.

But it was Nefertiti who commanded the most attention. Her crown was different to any I'd ever seen. It rose from her head at a sharp angle, broadening outwards to a flat top and was embellished with bands of lapis lazuli and carnelian. A golden cobra coiled at her forehead ready to spit its fiery venom into the eyes of her enemies and another cobra looped down from the side and hung against her cheek. The crown was the colour of the river on a clear day, and even from this distance drew green from her dark eyes. The stark outline of it, worn with her shaven head, drew attention to her high cheekbones and long, unadorned neck. A gossamer-thin tunic left one shoulder entirely bare while the other arm was covered by a full sleeve of fine pleats. Her tiny waist was clasped by a broad girdle embellished with the Sky Goddess, Nut, raising protective wings of blue glass and carnelian against a gold background.

There was no mistaking the full impact she made on the people of Thebes. With their eyes out on stalks, the men all goggling and the women all longing for a touch of her beauty, they cheered and applauded while the oarsmen dipped their oars rhythmically and the barge moved forward as steadily and stealthily as a crocodile's silent passage.

Nefertiti's brilliant image remained emblazoned on my eye long after the barge had disappeared around a bend in the river. And her distinctive heady perfume of lilies and bergamot and secret blends lingered and drifted above the water long afterwards.

There was no mistaking her power.

CHAPTER SEVEN

THE PRISON – TA-MIU

Jealousy is something that eats at you. It makes you fiercely protective and afraid and suspicious of rivalry in love. Intense. Resentful. Intolerant. And at all times vigilant. Nefertiti could not get rid of Kiya but she rid herself of me and in that way scored a victory over Kiya. *I* should have been more vigilant. Yet I trusted Samut. And now? How would I get out of this prison and prove my innocence without revealing his guilt?

'There you go! You're writing again. I can hear you. Scratch. Scratch. Scratch. Mark up the days and leave it be. He's not coming, is he? Believe me. Take an old woman's advice. How many days has it been now, deary? You might as well get used to being here. He's not going to come.'

A pestilence of flies on the woman! What did she want from me? As if I could protest. What could I say?

I looked at the few words I'd carved into the hard-baked mud-brick wall. The strokes were uneven. The point of the ankh didn't make a good stylus. But if I never left this cell, they would be a record. The ramblings of a servant who once lived at the Palace. A girl from Naharin. Maid to the Princess Tadukhepa. But she had trusted a boy. A boy with great charm.

I didn't carve his name. That way no one would know. The old woman in the cell next door was right. They were only marks on a blank surface. Meaningless scratches.

But Isis kept her brother, Osiris, alive only by remembering him. If I could just keep Samut alive, he would come. And as for me . . . if he didn't come? Words wouldn't help keep *me* alive. By the time someone read this, I would be long dead.

'You're very silent this morning. Are you keeping your strength up? It doesn't help to get weak. The bread they bring us is stale and the goat meat stringy. But you need to eat. I knew one girl who . . .'

Keep quiet, old woman! I wanted to shout. Instead,

I clenched my teeth and clutched my fingers around the ankh and began gouging out words in the hard-baked wall again. My hands were rough and cracked and there was dirt under my nails. My tears and sweat mixed and left dark streaks against the hard mud.

It was pointless. I jabbed the ankh into the wall.

Why? *Why* won't he come? *Where* is he? *Why* has he left me here to rot?

'Ah, I can hear you've started up again.'

Samut takes me to places I'd never seen before. We go by donkey to the tomb workers' village at the Place of Maat set far back from the Great River where, in the late afternoon, the steady *chink chink* of anvils comes from alleyways leading off behind the houses along the main street. And stonemasons send up clouds of dust that mix with the dust from the potters' wheels and the air is filled with the pungent smell of elm-wood shavings from the chariot makers' chisels. But when they all go off to work in the tombs, the village is silent except for the women and children.

Sometimes we walk out into the fields and sit in the shade of palm trees, the shadows so dense they seem black against the brilliant sunlight, or find a deserted ruin of a courtyard with a shady mimosa or pomegranate tree.

Samut teases and brings words bubbling out of me. Draws them from me, as if my heart is a huge, red, flaring poppy that opens and opens and opens in the warm sunshine.

I tell him of the journey from Mitanni. Of the heat and dust. Of how Kiya is wrenched from the arms of her mother. Of how she weeps and clings to me as we are carried in our palanquin on that beastly camel, down the high mountains and across the plains and along the banks of the Khabur River accompanied by a thousand horsemen, until we come to the crossing place on the mighty Euphrates River.

A thousand horsemen? Samut smiles as if he doesn't believe me. But there were. And eventually we sail from Tyre across an ocean so wide there is no end to it and enter Egypt where the sea sips up the waters of the Great River.

Forty of the three hundred serving girls die along the way from stomach ailments and lack of fresh water. Kiya's father, Tushratta, cares nothing for our discomfort or his daughter's young age. All he considers is winning the respect and acknowledgement of King Amenhotep. If you send me gold, he writes, I will give you my daughter. Send me as much as you are able. In your country gold is like dust. You gather it up in armfuls.

King Amenhotep died during our journey, long before we even reached Thebes.

And Kiya is passed on to his son, Tuthmosis, without ever having laid eyes on the King she has been sent to in the first place. When we arrive we huddle, wretched and homesick, in front of the vizier of the court as he inspects our gifts of golden chariots and our beasts laden with chests of treasure and flagous of oil, while scribes list all we have brought, as well as all we have not brought.

Twenty chariots with six-spoked wheels
One hundred trained chariot horses
Thirty experienced horse handlers
Forty alabaster jars of myrrh
One hundred sheep pelts worked to a fine softness
Three hundred baby lamb skins
One hundred finely-woven wool blankets
Four chests of nuggets of lapis lazuli known as khesbed
One chest of silver bars known as hedj
Ten jars of pine kernel oil
Five jars of sef wan oil extracted from the wood of the
Syrian juniper
Twenty bags of ginger root
Ten bags of the finest pine resin for making kapet to
burn in the temple

Thirty jars of sweet bak oil from Naharin for perfume
and cosmetics
Nekfitir oil from Sangar for anointing
Gati oil from Takhsi for anointing

The list goes on and on and when the scribes
have finally recorded the last gift, we ourselves are
inspected and prodded. Kiya has to undergo the
humiliation of having her body stripped and assized
by various women who cluck at her youthful appearance and lack of breasts and skinny arms. Finally it
is her aunt, Princess Gilukhipa, who had arrived at
the Palace of Thebes twenty-six years before and
has privilege and status beyond many of the others,
who chases them away and demands we be treated
properly.

'You've started again. I wish I knew what it is you're
writing. You're so silent but I can feel the heat of your
words even if you don't say them aloud. You should
rest now, deary. I can hear your sighs. Leave off all this
scratching. Close your eyes and sleep.'
    Sleep? I wish I could.

I lie in Samut's arms. While I tell my stories, he
touches the ankh key that hangs around my neck

alongside the glass scarab he has given me.

I've given you my heart in the shape of this scarab, why do you insist on still wearing that ankh? Who gave it to you? Whose heart does the ankh key unlock?

Yes, jealousy makes people fiercely protective and afraid and suspicious of rivalry in love. Resentful. Intolerant, even.

I don't tell him that it was Tuthmosis who gave me the ankh key when I helped him escape Thebes. He gave it to me in case there was ever any need for me to hide. But when I was thrown into prison there'd been no time to use it. Nor do I tell him that it was Tuthmosis who persuaded me to have my shoulder tattooed with the little cat. And that it was he who first gave me the name Ta-Miu.

All this I keep silent about.

Instead, I shake my head. *The ankh key unlocks no heart, Samut.*

What then?

A gate, I answer.

What gate?

It's a secret.

But jealousy makes people vigilant too. His lips brush against my cheek. He whispers close to my ear. *You will tell it to me in your dreams. I will draw it from you like a bee draws essence from a flower.*

Don't be silly, Samut. It's just an amulet. A key shaped like an ankh.

He keeps his face so close I have to shut my eyes to steady myself. He takes my cheeks in his hands and drops kisses on my eyelids. And then his lips are searching mine. And my body is filled with such heat and giddiness. So warm and wonderful are his kisses, I lose all thought of who I am and where we are and cling to him.

And much later I ask him about himself.

He shrugs. *There's nothing to tell.*

Stop teasing, Samut. That's not true. What are those marks on your arms? Are you a falconer?

Perhaps I'm a tomb robber, after all, as Kiya said. A tomb robber who robs the rich and gives away the jewels and gold to friends. He smiles close, right into my eyes as he speaks.

I laugh back at him. *The tombs are well-guarded. You'd never get past the guards. And even if you did, you'd never find your way to the central chambers because of all the trapdoors and secret passageways with false doors.*

But a tomb robber? Can it be true? Would Samut ever dare enter the tomb of a dead King? Everyone knows about the wealth the tombs contain. But everyone knows the wealth is for the Afterlife and that inscriptions warn robbers that they will be judged by

76

the gods and cursed forever for committing such a terrible crime as tomb robbing!

It is unthinkable that he would dare.

CHAPTER EIGHT

THE GODDESS HATHOR

When I came to the Temple, there was the usual group of old women sweeping the front steps with mimosa branches to ward off the evils of the day. They shook their branches at the urchin boys playing catch around them. 'Be off with you! A plague on your parents for breeding such pests!'

As I passed by, one of the women sucked at her teeth and nodded in my direction. 'Look, there she is again! That girl! An offering made every day this week to the goddess, Hathor. I know a moonstruck girl when I see one!'

They seemed a little deaf. Perhaps a little blind even. Couldn't they tell I heard every word they said? One of them leant on her mimosa branch and cackled out loud. 'What do you know about being moonstruck, old Meryt?'

'I might look as old and worn as the treads on these stone steps, but I've done my fair share of making offerings before Hathor with a heart full of longing.'

'And look what it got you!'

'Yes, an old goat of a husband! But there were plenty of handsome boys before him.'

'By the white feather of Maat, that's true!' one of the women sighed. 'We've all had our share of handsome boys running after us. But those days are long gone now. And *my* old goat has gone to the Afterlife. Horus bless him!'

'Perhaps that's all we can hope for, Senen. A new lover in our Afterlife.'

The remark brought about a fresh bout of cackling until finally they were bent over double, heaving and wheezing so badly, they could hardly catch their breath.

'To be fair, we should warn this girl that Hathor doesn't always bring us the right lover on this earth. The Goddess of Love is full of tricks and surprises!'

'Yes, and even the fine young men Hathor sends us get old and end up eventually as goats!'

As I went up the steps they dropped their voices down to whispers, but even these were loud enough to wake the dead. One of them nodded in my direction. 'Have you seen who she's after? She meets every afternoon with that boy with the face too handsome for his own good.'

'Hmm! A lazy boy that one, if you ask me!'

You were not asked . . . I wanted to snap back but bit my tongue. It was idle gossip.

'They say he comes from the workers' village at the Place of Maat. But I've never seen him do a day's work. How does he get by? Why would a boy of such good health and such bodily strength not be working?'

'Been ogling him, have you then, Meryt?'

'A frog in your mouth, Senen, for speaking such nonsense!'

'Meryt's right. Never seen him lift a bag of barley. Never seen him get his hands dirty. A proper layabout, is he!'

'And a lady's man too, if all his flirting with that girl is anything to go by. Seen the two of them kissing down the alleyways.'

'Not getting many kisses yourself in the alleyways, then, Meryt?'

'Ah, get on with you! Wouldn't let my daughter carry on like that. But the girl seems not to have family in Thebes. Not sure where she comes from.'

'Foreign, I'd say! She was at the market the same time as the Syrian traders. Perhaps she's one of them. She has that dark, foreign look.'

I stood before the more-than-life-size statue of Hathor and blocked my ears to their chatter. 'Oh Hathor, Goddess of Love, Celestial Goddess, Mistress of Heaven, Goddess of Women, you have filled me with longing,' I whispered as I placed the rush basket of ripened figs at her feet. I had chosen the figs with as much care as if they were to be broken open and offered as fleshy morsels to the very lips of Samut. The sweet lushness of sun-ripened figs was said to draw love from a lover. Hathor knew about love. I glanced up to see if she was listening.

'Hathor, Goddess of Love, Celestial Goddess, Goddess of Women, accept my offering.'

Did I imagine a smile twitching around her mouth in answer?

I couldn't bluff Kiya. She knew I was going across the river every afternoon. After it happened for the fourth time, she grinned at me as she lined up a row of dead flies for her chameleon. 'What do you do there and *who* do you see?'

'Stop teasing, Kiya.'

'But what shall I say if you're missed?'

'Say I've gone to the Palace library. No one ever goes there.'

'The library! What would you be studying?'

'Stop teasing! Tell them anything. Just make up a story. Tell them Nefertiti has sent me to her Unguent Rooms to learn the art of perfume-making.'

Kiya laughed. 'That would be as unlikely a story as the library!'

The women were right. I *was* moonstruck. Completely caught in Hathor's web. She had woven a tight net of moonbeams around me that clung to my body as closely as a beaded dress. At night when I couldn't sleep, I found myself roaming the Palace gardens thinking of the afternoon I'd just spent with Samut and already longing for the next afternoon so I could feel his hot kisses along my neck and have his arms around me.

Never mind Tuthmosis now. All thought of him had evaporated as quickly as a pool of water on a hot day. He could be in Nubia with that girl from the crocodile Temple, for all I cared. It was Samut I loved.

CHAPTER NINE

THE PALACE STABLES

A shadow moves through the gardens. The night is moonless. Dark as a deep river pool and just as silent.

A sharp sound breaks the silence. The shadow stops and waits as still and silent as a cypress.

Footsteps approach. It's a guard on patrol. His leather boots make scratching sounds against the gravel scattered on the stone pathway. The gardeners have not been diligent enough in their sweeping. The sound can be heard far into the distance after the guard has passed. Then silence as the guard steps off the pathway and the soft earth takes his footsteps into the night.

Safe then, the shadow moves forward again along pathways he knows well. He keeps his distance from the flares lighting every niche and archway of the Palace and avoids the lake lit up with floating lamps and the glow of light hovering above it. He keeps to more closed sections of the garden where roses dark as blood cloud the air with perfume and, in a sudden breeze, pale lilies are sails in a sea of penumbral blackness.

Instinctively he knows the route the guard has taken. The short cut through the planted courtyard towards the stables. There he will meet another guard coming from the other direction. If the evening is slightly cold they will stamp their feet and rub their hands and pull their wool cloaks about them and chat quickly before moving briskly on.

Tonight is warm. Sultry even. Tonight they will linger. Maybe even lounge against a pillar and chat about their girlfriends or tell of a backstreet beer-room brawl where a man was stabbed for looking at another man's wife.

Guards have no fear of men with daggers. They are trained to kill. But tonight killing is far from the mind of the first guard. He has come from the kitchen with his stomach full of the freshly-baked bread the baker's assistant has given him and his mouth still warm from her dough-fresh kisses.

The two guards lean up against the pillars and their

voices drift quietly into the sultry night. They don't notice as the shadow slips silently past them. Now he must move quickly and avoid the animal cages. If the monkeys are disturbed and start to howl they will bring the dogs running. He knows the way. Even in the darkness his feet are sure of the path.

Now the stables are ahead. He smells the warm aroma of barley and straw mixed with the animal smell of muck and horses' breath.

For a moment he pauses. Tempted by the need to run his hands over the flanks of a horse. To brush one down. Still now he knows the training schedule passed on to him by the Mitannian horse handler. He can recite it exactly in his head – the precise order of rotating trotting with cantering over exact distances with the animal in harness, to strengthen the legs and the heart of the horse. The action long, low and economical, with little bend or lift in the knee. The short rest between to relax the horse partially before another round. And the exact proportion of oats to barley and chaff in the morning, midday and evening feeds. And after the training every one of the horses brushed down and cooled off and washed in warm water and rugged.

A stable cat scavenging for mice in the straw runs mewing towards him and rubs up against his legs. A horse whinnies. There is the sound of a door scraping. A stable hand moves about whistling under his breath, hanging things up, moving brooms, kicking leather buckets into place. The stable hand clears his throat and hawks some phlegm. Then slams the heavy door. The sound of footfalls disappears into the night.

He stands well back against a wall and makes sure the stable hand won't think of something he has forgotten and turn back.

He knows there are two new horses. They've come from the king of Assyria. Horses as white as freshly-washed linen. Whiter than the moon. It would be safe to enter the stables now. But he daren't. He can't linger tonight. There are important things to accomplish before the goddess Nut draws the sun into the sky again. He must do what needs to be done and return before a vestige of light creeps across the sky.

He moves on. A shadow disappearing swiftly into the darkness.

CHAPTER TEN

ANUBIS – JACKAL OF DEATH

Even without moonlight, he sees the place ahead.

When he's near the gate, he checks over his shoulder to see no one has followed. Then he fumbles along the stone wall, feeling for a shelf or niche just inside the gate that he knows must be there, and finds what he is looking for. He slips the ankh key into place and hears the click of metal moving against metal. With a push, the gate swings stiffly inwards into a space as dark as a hyena's mouth.

Now, for the first time, he hesitates. He fumbles with unwrapping the small clay lamp he has carried in his girdle bag. Then he pulls the gate closed behind and hears the lock click. He waits for his eyes to grow accustomed to the gloom, then takes a sharp breath and steps into the darkness as one would plunge into a deep pool. A few paces beyond, where the flame can't be seen, he lights the lamp. He has soaked the linen wick and put salt in the oil to prevent it from smoking too much. Now, he holds the lamp high so its glow extends far into the distance, but he can see no end to the vast tunnel ahead.

He shuffles forward, searching the walls with his fingers, tracing over the stone at the entrance to every new passageway, searching for indents he knows will be there to mark the correct passage. Three notches each time, is what the girl has said. They are hard to find. Sometimes his fingers as well as his eyes mislead him and he needs to retrace his steps.

Suddenly something looms up. He wants to cry out but the silence presses down on him like a weight that holds him paralysed.

Anubis stands towering over him, his jackal face dark and his eyes intense as burning embers, carrying an ankh, the symbol of life, in his left hand. The silence is broken by a soft growl, light as a falling feather, yet it fills the whole chamber with sound.

Follow me, Anubis beckons.

On an altar, a small fire is burning. He can smell the scent of cedar-wood. He blinks. Is this truly happening?

Anubis scatters white powder into the flame. A ball of fire leaps up with a swish, then sinks into darkness again. The deep voice of Anubis rumbles through the chamber like thunder and the rock echoes with his growls.

I will release your soul so it can fly into the World of the Dead, and see all that happens there. Swifter than light, we will travel above the Ferry-Boat of Ra as it sails up the river to the World of the Dead. There Thoth waits in the Hall of Maat with the Scales of Justice. Pay attention. Time is short. We must be back before morning if you want to live to see the Sun of Ra rise over Egypt.

Suddenly the rock overhead splits open. He feels himself flying upwards – a great bird on huge, beating wings with golden feathers, his own head emerging from the winged shoulders.

The world is in darkness beneath him. The Great River is nothing but a narrow, silver ribbon winding through a silent landscape of temples no larger than small, mud bricks. Thebes is a city scraped out of mud and dust by a child's hand. Even the colossal statues of King Amenhotep guarding either side of his Mortuary Temple can be scooped up in each hand. Palm fronds are small as the breast feathers of a dove and sleeping cows in fields no larger than ticks on the back of a dog.

They are speeding into the West through the shadowy dip of Abydos in the mountains, swifter than arrows from a Kushite's bow-string. Below them is the splendid gold Boat of Ra, glowing with jewels of amethyst, emerald, turquoise and lapis lazuli. A company of gods is drawing the boat along a ghostly River of Death with golden tow-ropes. The boat is filled with the souls of all who have died that day. He shudders as he recognises some faces. There is the old woman who baked honey cakes and there is his neighbour's grandfather.

They are exact doubles of their earthly bodies.

They speed onwards and the gates of the World of the Dead are flung wide. Six writhing snakes, thicker than a man's leg, are curled on either side of the gate, breathing fire and poison. But they must pass through to where Osiris stands waiting to receive them.

He hears the Door-Keeper challenge them. *I will not announce thee unless you know my name!*

Understander of Hearts is your name! they reply.

To whom must I announce thee? demands the Door-Keeper.

To the Interpreter of the Two Lands, Thoth, the God of Wisdom.

So each soul passes through the doorway.

In the Hall, Thoth stands waiting with his sharp,

curved Ibis beak and his hand poised ready to write their names on his writing tablet. *Why have you come?* he asks each one in turn.

I am pure of sin, each replies.

Thoth leads them to where Osiris sits upon his throne, wrapped in the green mummy-clothes of the dead, wearing the spitting cobra upon his forehead and holding the scourge and the crook crossed upon his breast. Before him is a huge balance with two dishes shaped like gigantic fish scales – the Scales of Justice. Next to this stands Maat, Goddess of Justice, Truth and Order, wearing a white feather on her head. And crouched low on the ground is the terrible monster, Ammut, Devourer of the Dead, with an upper body of a crocodile, the middle of a lion, and the hind-quarters of a hippopotamus. The terrible stench of her breath cannot be masked as she waits to snatch hearts that weigh too heavy.

Now, suddenly, the jackal-headed Anubis, God of Death, swoops towards him.

No! You're mistaken! I'm not truly dead. Remember! You said we must be back before the morning, to see the Sun of Ra rise again over Egypt. I'm not here to be judged.

You will be judged if you enter this tomb! Anubis growls.

Now he panics. He tries to think of the proper

incantations. The spells that are written on papyrus and placed in every dead person's coffin. But he *isn't* dead. This is surely a dream.

Say them! Anubis's eyes glow in the flickering lamplight. *Say them, or Ammut will devour you!*

Ammut, Devourer of the Dead, crouches ready to destroy him with her drooling lips and treacherous teeth. He tries to speak but his tongue is thick in his mouth. The words won't come. His mouth won't open.

Anubis's eyes glow like burning embers.

Ammut bears her teeth. Her snout is bloody.

I have not disobeyed the gods, he shouts at last. *I have not stolen from the dead. I have not inflicted pain on anyone. I have not killed.*

Not yet! Anubis's dark jackal head swings from side to side. *But you have been warned!*

Suddenly, everything vanishes. He is standing alone in the dark, empty chamber, giddy with what he has just experienced. The hideous Ammut has gone, and with her, Osiris, Maat and Thoth. The heavy weight of the golden wings has dropped from his shoulders. His body is suddenly weak as if his kneecaps have dissolved. His legs are unable to hold him upright.

He blinks hard. Where is Anubis? Has he dreamt it all?

Before him a sandal is wedged in the crevice of a rock, holding open a secret door. He has no time to think who has left it there. He pushes the door. It swings slowly on its pivot of stone. On the other side, carved in black obsidian, is a silent statue of Anubis, sitting with his forelegs stretched out in front of him, guarding the deep well and the secret passage to the King's tomb. His jackal ears stand sharply upwards. His eyes look straight ahead. His body is silent as stone.

He must still his heart. This Anubis is nothing to be feared.

He must do what he has come to do.

CHAPTER ELEVEN

THE SCALES OF JUSTICE

'Hurry, Kiya! Stop playing with that chameleon. Put it back in its cage. Be quick now. Nefertiti has summoned us.'

Kiya sighed as she returned the chameleon to its branch. 'The robe you've chosen for me is boring. Can't I wear the cloth you bought at the market?'

I shook my head. 'Let me look at you. Let's see you haven't broken any of Nefertiti's rules. Don't forget to remove your sandals in her presence. In the company of Nefertiti only she, who has no earthly superiors, can wear sandals. We must have our wits about us and pray to Thoth, God of Wisdom, that he'll put the right words in our mouths when the time comes to speak.'

Kiya pulled at her tunic.

'Stop fidgeting, Kiya. Let the song of your Golden Oriole soothe you.'

'The bird doesn't soothe me today. I'm anxious.'

'There's nothing to be anxious about.'

Kiya raised her eyebrow. 'Then why are we being summoned, Ta-Miu?'

'The messenger didn't say. All he said was Nefertiti wanted a private audience with you and I should accompany you.'

I saw the little panicky stars of worry in Kiya's eyes. 'What if she's found out you've been crossing the Great River and meeting with Samut?'

'How?'

'A boatman might've discovered your identity and reported you.'

I shook my head. 'I've bribed the boatmen with figs and pomegranates from my offering basket. And I've told them I'm a relative of one of the potters from the Place of Maat. Samut explained some of their methods and the pigments they use for colourants. If I'm questioned it'll seem as if I've lived all my life in the workers' village and been brought up in a family of potters.'

'Then *why* are we being summoned?'

I shrugged. 'With Nefertiti there could be any number of reasons.'

When we reached her quarters, we were shown to an antechamber outside her Receiving Rooms.

'Nefertiti is busy with her offering rites,' we were told by an attendant.

Through the colonnades we caught a glimpse of her in a simple tunic under the canopy of her private temple, holding her hands up in obeisance and whispering incantations and prayers. When she had completed her ritual, she approached and took in our appearance with a quick, scathing glance.

'Wait here,' she commanded, 'while I remove my temple robes.' Then she strode to her chambers and we were left with nothing to do but stand and wait for her return.

I saw Kiya bite her lip. I reached out to squeeze her hand. 'Don't worry. Making us wait is part of her plan.' But I was anxious and nervous too. I'd been reckless in meeting Samut and now Kiya was involved. Why else were we being summoned?

Outside, there was a sound of quick footsteps and the door of the anteroom was flung open. The Chief Vizier rushed into the room. 'We have it!' he announced to some attendants. 'Hurry! Tell the Queen!'

Kiya and I looked at each other, totally mystified.

Clearly it was an important announcement as Amenhotep the Younger and the Highest of High Priests, Wosret, made a quick entrance behind the Chief Vizier. Attendants swept the floor with mimosa branches before them and sprinkled the air with oils and swung their censers of burning incense so vigorously I thought I would choke and Kiya started sneezing.

Nefertiti emerged from her robing room bejewelled in queenly regalia with her new, towering, turquoise crown, accompanied by her fan-bearers and the two cheetahs.

Amenhotep and Wosret strode past us through the antechamber and led her to her Receiving Room. We were hurried along behind them amidst wafts of incense that had Kiya sneezing all the way. Amenhotep helped Nefertiti step onto a dais and be seated on her gold lion-footed throne. The three of them conferred in whispers before calling the Chief Vizier forward.

All this was done without anyone speaking a word to us. So little attention was paid us, I found myself counting the moments between Kiya's sneezes. And then my mind wandered to the ostrich feather fans with their long, dark ebony handles held by two small attendants and the detail of the throne with its intricate ivory patterns of flying herons and its high, carved back lustred with gold leaf, in the shape of a sun with rays shining down on Nefertiti seated below. The throne was so impressive that, despite her tall crown, she appeared small against its grandeur. She sat too high for her legs to reach the ground and her feet rested on a plump red-cushioned footstool. I stared, fascinated, at her sandals in fine leather with thongs of delicate gold filigree, adorned with daisies and lotus lilies of lapis lazuli with tiny ducks peering out from behind them.

Despite my nervousness I couldn't help smiling at the ducks. Thank goodness Kiya and I had remembered to remove our sandals at the door.

Suddenly Wosret turned and faced Kiya. His dark eyes flashed. 'We have a serious accusation against your maid.'

The suddenness of the announcement stopped Kiya's sneezes immediately. I felt my stomach clench. So this *was* about me!

Kiya pulled herself up as tall as she could, before replying, 'I'm ready to hear your accusation, my Lord.'

'This girl,' he pointed at me, 'has been an accomplice to theft of the highest order.'

I took a step forward but Kiya put out a hand to stop me. 'Theft?' She shook her head. 'Ta-Miu's not a thief! What are you speaking of?'

I held my breath, knowing the protocol of court. I was not allowed to speak unless directly addressed by Nefertiti, Amenhotep or Wosret. And until I was spoken to, I couldn't open my mouth, let alone *question* anything they said.

'Why do you accuse her unjustly?'

'Unjustly?' His eyes raked across me as if I was as unclean as the lowliest of beggars, as if for his eyes to rest on me, they would immediately be contaminated with some awful disease. 'It's *she* who has caused injustice. She's stolen from Egypt.'

'Stolen? *What* has she stolen?'

'She knows the labyrinth that leads from the Palace grounds to King Amenhotep's tomb.'

'King Amenhotep's tomb? But what has—'

'Everyone in the Palace knows she was on more than friendly terms with Prince Tuthmosis who knew the labyrinth like the lines on the palm of his hand. The Chief Vizier here can vouch for how well Tuthmosis knew it. As a boy, he spent hours playing there when it was being built.'

'You forget Ta-Miu is my closest handmaiden. I would know if there was something between them that was more than friendship. You forget I was betrothed to Tuthmosis after his father died, and would have married him myself.'

'Your betrothal doesn't mean that your hand-maiden was above planning to run away with him.'

I couldn't stop myself. 'That's not *true*.'

Wosret's eyes bore into me. 'Silence! How *dare* you speak!'

Kiya pulled at my tunic and hissed, 'Hush, Ta-Miu. I will deal with this.'

It was odd to have our roles reversed. To have her telling me what to do.

Wosret nodded at Amenhotep. 'The two of them, Tuthmosis and this girl, planned this together. They entered the labyrinth after the burial of your father, the King, and stole his treasure.'

Amenhotep raised his eyebrows. 'What? That's absurd. What proof have you, Wosret?'

'They needed gold and jewels to be able to pay their way so Tuthmosis could escape.'

'*Escape*? But my brother Tuthmosis is dead. This story makes no sense, Wosret! You led me to believe my brother died of grief at my mother's death.'

Wosret waved his hand in the air as if he was hurrying some tardy assistant. 'Yes . . . yes . . . that's so. That's what *I* believed at the time. That your brother had died. It's what we *all* believed. It's what we were all *led* to believe by that traitor Henuka, who was present at your mother's embalming. *Henuka* told us Tuthmosis had died. But it's been suggested Tuthmosis is alive.'

'*Alive? Impossible!*' Amenhotep shook his head. 'Why haven't you told me this before?'

'We had no proof. I didn't want to disturb you. But now the truth is out because of the discovery of this theft. This serving girl helped Tuthmosis steal your father's riches. She helped him plunder his own father's tomb and then escape up the river to Nubia.'

Kiya stepped forward. 'By the white feather of Maat, your story doesn't fit with mine.'

'Be silent! We are here to discuss your maid's treachery.'

Amenhotep looked searchingly at Wosret. 'It doesn't make sense. Why would my brother steal from my father's tomb, if he was to be King of Egypt himself? He had no need of all that wealth.'

Wosret shrugged. 'I'm sorry you have to discover the truth this way. Your brother didn't want to be King. He was a traitor. I would have preferred it if he were truly dead. I would have preferred you to think well of him. But you didn't know him as I did. He was devious. He stole because he needed the wealth to build up an army against Egypt.'

'An army *against* Egypt? Have you lost your mind? What proof have you?'

All this time Nefertiti had remained silent. Now suddenly she thrust her hand forward and spoke. 'This!'

I gasped. In the cup of her hand was a ring with an emerald so huge, it sparked green against her palm. Could it be the same ring? There was no mistaking that huge green stone. Yet the ring Samut had given me the day before was safely buried under my bedlinen. I'd slept with it under my pillow all night, feeling the lump of it, and had hidden it beneath my pallet this morning.

'That's my father's ring!' Amenhotep snatched it up from Nefertiti's hand and held it to the light. He glanced quickly at her. 'What connection is there between my father's ring and this girl from Naharin?'

'She helped Tuthmosis steal it. She kept it after he left.'

What? I clenched Kiya's hand and looked from one to another. *That's not true!* I wanted to shout out. *The ring has* nothing *to do with Tuthmosis.*

Kiya shook her head. 'Impossible! I've never seen this ring before.'

Wosret nodded. '*You* wouldn't have. It belonged to King Amenhotep. It was buried with him after his death along with all his other treasures for the Afterlife. But the tomb has been broken into, the treasures scattered, the best taken – nothing as large as the golden chariots of course – but the smaller valuables have all disappeared. The chests of lapis lazuli, the jewel-encrusted daggers, the goblets and gold statues, the jewellery, are gone. The Chief Vizier can attest to this. He has a record of everything that was buried with the King and has drawn up a list of everything that is missing – stolen from right under the gaze of Anubis, Jackal of the Underworld, and the Cobra Goddess. Who but the son of a King would *dare*? This robbery was planned by Tuthmosis.' Wosret glared around at each person. Complete silence descended as everyone took in his words.

Kiya's voice broke the silence. 'This has *nothing* to do with Ta-Miu.'

I could not believe her bravery.

Wosret's eyes darted over her. 'Your maid was Tuthmosis's close friend. She knew his plans. She helped him escape on the day of the Opet festival when everyone was at the Temple of Amun. What better proof than finding this distinctive emerald ring in her possession? There's no other ring like it.'

Kiya shook her head. 'I've never seen her with it.'

Nefertiti narrowed her eyes and looked directly at Kiya. 'Nor would you! You're just a child. What would you know of such things? Your maid is devious! She kept it hidden from you. But one of my ladies saw it on her finger out in the garden last night. She noticed the incredible dazzle of the emerald in the moonlight. No other gem would reflect such sparkle. While we kept you waiting here, we searched her quarters and found it tucked under her bedlinen. We need no further proof.'

Kiya turned to glance at me, her eyes begging me to be innocent of this.

Wosret nodded. 'She's guilty of tomb robbery. She's defiled the King's tomb. If King Amenhotep is not properly received into the Afterlife, it'll be *her* doing. She has defiled the sanctity of his tomb.'

'*No . . .!*' I couldn't stop myself.

'Be silent! You're not addressed!'

Kiya tugged hurriedly at my tunic and managed to keep her voice calm. 'You're mistaken, my Queen. The ring must have been placed there by someone else. If Ta-Miu was guilty of tomb robbery, I'd know. I know all her secrets. She has been at my side since we were children.'

Nefertiti surveyed Kiya coldly. One perfectly-plucked eyebrow lifted high into the dark curve of a kestrel's wing. 'If that is so, then you would know where she's been going when she leaves the Palace every afternoon.'

I heard Kiya's sharp intake of breath. 'How can you possibly know?'

'So you *do* admit she leaves the Palace? We were suspicious and put a guard on her but she's managed each time to lose him.'

'This has *nothing* to do with the ring. My Lord,' Kiya turned to Amenhotep, 'allow my maid to speak for herself.'

Amenhotep nodded. 'Let's hear her, then.'

Wosret held the ring beneath my face. 'Do you know this ring?'

'I believe it was one King Amenhotep wore.'

'Answer directly. Have you seen this ring before?

I swallowed hard. How could I explain without telling them it was Samut who had given it to me? I nodded. 'I have.'

Kiya's eyebrows shot up. She clutched my arm. 'You couldn't possibly have, Ta-Miu. What are you saying? Please tell me it was placed under your pallet by someone else.'

Nefertiti regarded us coolly. 'Clearly your maid is

not as innocent as you believe. Not only has she seen it but she's also worn it. Is that not so?'

I shook my head and then nodded. 'I . . . I can't deny this. But . . .'

Kiya gripped my hand. 'Ta-Miu, I beg you. You're *mistaken*.'

I couldn't meet Kiya's eyes. I looked down at the floor and noticed for the first time the pattern of herons and lotus lilies that floated across it, in a scene of peace far removed from this turmoil. 'I'd like to say I'm mistaken . . . but I'm *not*.'

Wosret's eyes flashed triumphantly. 'Did you steal it from the labyrinth yourself?'

I shook my head.

'Then how do you come to possess it?'

I thought of the day before . . . could it only be the day before? . . . of what I'd said to Samut, when I first laid eyes on the ring.

I can't possibly accept another gift from you! Not one so large! The jewel is the size of a pigeon's egg.

A girl as beautiful as you deserves nothing better, he'd answered.

We were sitting in the shade of the pomegranate tree in our crumbling courtyard on the outskirts of the city. Even in the shade the jewel sparked and

106

sent flashes of green fire against my skin. I'd been breathless with excitement.

Samut closed my fingers over the ring and whispered, *It's the fire burning in my heart. Keep it, Ta-Miu.*

But I can never wear something as grand as this.

It's not for you to wear. Keep it hidden and look at it when we're not together to remind you of me. Let it take the place of the ankh given you by that prince!

I hid the ring in my girdle bag all the way home. Then last night as I walked in the gardens, I'd taken it out and placed it on my thumb, the only finger it fitted, and watched the moonlight sending sparks of green fire through it.

Now Wosret was asking me again, his voice insisting. But I *couldn't* say Samut had given it to me. I couldn't bring his name into this. How could I admit I'd told him about the labyrinth gate and that my ankh key was a duplicate of a key kept just inside the gate? I couldn't accuse him on such small grounds. I didn't know for sure.

Would he have entered the tomb? I had to ask him first. He'd surely have a reason for how he had acquired the ring. He wasn't a tomb robber. He'd been joking when he said he was. Someone had given it to him. A jeweller friend. Maybe the ring was a copy.

'Answer me!' Wosret demanded.

I shook my head. 'I . . . I . . . can't say!'

Wosret put his face close to mine, so close I smelt the garlic on his breath. 'You *can't*? You mean you *will* not!'

'I'm sure it's a copy. It can't be the real ring.'

'How would a mere maid know the difference between a copy and the real ring? And besides, how did you get possession of a copy?'

'It was given me by a friend of a jeweller.'

Nefertiti raised an eyebrow. 'If it's a copy, why is the real ring missing from the tomb?'

Wosret nodded. 'There is only one answer. Tuthmosis stole it with all the other treasure that's missing from his father's tomb. This girl knew of the tomb robbery and to ensure her silence, Tuthmosis gave her the ring as his parting gift when he escaped with the rest of his father's treasure.'

Wosret's lizard eyes darted triumphantly over me. Then he turned to Amenhotep. 'I was right to appoint you as King in your brother's place. Tuthmosis is nothing but a foul tomb robber and this girl is no better, as his accomplice.'

Amenhotep raised his hand. 'Wosret, until we have proven this, I ask you *not* to accuse my brother of theft.'

Wosret bowed. 'Believe me, sir, you are young and have been protected from the evils that lie beyond the Palace walls. Let me handle this. This girl must be imprisoned for life for such treachery.'

'No . . .!' Kiya's voice sounded strangled. 'Please, my Lord, I beg you!' She fell at Amenhotep's feet.

Wosret cut across her words. 'Get up at once. You have no say in this!'

Amenhotep touched Kiya's shoulder. 'Let Princess Tadukhepa speak. She is entitled!'

'*Entitled?*' Nefertiti stood up so briskly that the amethysts swinging from her ears jangled as they caught the light and her eyes matched their flare. 'Entitled by what? No, Amenhotep! Listen to me, your First Royal Wife. She can't be trusted. She tried to protect her maid and denies what we've discovered, which is unforgivable. We don't have to listen to her. Tadukhepa's a mere child! And a foreign child at that!'

'Nefertiti, stop speaking such harsh words. We must be as fair and wise as Thoth weighing the Scales of Justice. We must hear all sides before we come to a conclusion. Princess Tadukhepa's maid will be held in prison until we know the *exact* truth. Then, if she's innocent, she'll be set free.'

I heard Kiya's sharp intake of breath. '*Prison? Not prison!*'

And my own heart turned to stone. I was to be held captive . . . until I was proved innocent. But who could prove me innocent?

PART TWO

CHAPTER TWELVE

THE TEMPLE OF SOBEK

Isikara sat up front in the reed boat with Tuthmosis behind her. The wind in her face brought with it a perfume of lotus lilies, reeds and damp earth. It had blown stiffly against them every day since they left Nubia. But even though the Great Flood had receded, the current was still strong enough to drive them downstream without need for strenuous paddling.

Now she felt a stirring of excitement like butterfly wings brushing against her throat. There was something enticing about getting back to places that were familiar. Her eyes feasted on the colour of the soil along the banks, the palm trees and mud houses, the donkeys and men tilling the rich, dark fields. It had been a long time. Too long!

'Look, Tuthmosis . . .' She pointed. 'There! Under those palms. That's the place where we slept on the first night of our escape after we'd met Wosret on the river, where we found ourselves in the path of that hippopotamus.'

'And you were terrified.'

'How would you know?' Isikara gave him a quick sidelong glance. 'You slept instead of protecting me!' Then she faced forward again. 'It's strange to be back. Do you think anyone will recognise us?'

'You don't look like the girl who left with me.'

'What did she look like?'

'She was fair-skinned. Pretty.'

'And?' She hit down hard with her paddle so that water drenched Tuthmosis. 'What am I now?'

He grabbed her arm and nearly tipped the boat. 'You're as sunburnt as a peasant girl who's worked in the fields all her life. Just as well. No one must recognise us. No one must know we've returned until I've spoken secretly to my brother. If Wosret gets a hint of us being in Thebes, he'll be after us. I might not live long enough to even draw breath, let alone speak to my brother. I don't trust him.'

'What will you tell your brother?'

'The truth. That his High Priest tried to poison me. That I know Wosret had ulterior motives for making him King instead of me.'

'He'll think you've come to take the throne from him.'

Tuthmosis shook his head. 'My brother's not a fool. He might be young but he's been influenced by my father. My father was always suspicious of the priests of Amun and their need to control. But he was powerful enough and they were scared enough of him not to step out of line. He believed more and more that Thebes should honour a single god.'

'Amun-Ra, the Sun-God?' Isikara shrugged. 'We *all* believe in him.'

Tuthmosis shook his head. 'Not Amun-Ra but Aten, the sun itself. Remember my father named the Royal Barge *Dazzling Aten*.'

Isikara stopped paddling and twisted around to stare at him. 'But no one can honour the sun directly. The priests would never allow it.'

'Exactly! That's why I must meet my brother so he can see how he's being manipulated by the priests. He must take away their control. If Aten is the god of Thebes, there'll be no need for the Priests of Amun. He can get rid of them.'

'What? That's unheard of! What will happen to the gods Amun, Mut and Khonsu?'

'They'll become unimportant.'

Isikara sucked in her breath. 'The three gods of Thebes? Unimportant? Are you serious? Wosret will *never* stand for it. Please, Tuthmosis, you *can't* speak out. They'll kill you for such treachery.'

'Protecting the throne isn't treachery! Wosret tried to murder me. The priests have been plotting for a long while to control Thebes. I *have* to meet my brother before Wosret discovers we've returned. Now keep paddling, Isikara, or we'll never get to the Place of Maat before nightfall.'

She looked over her shoulder at him. 'The Place of Maat? I thought we were going to the Palace so Ta-Miu could help us.'

'It's too risky. We'd be recognised. It's better to stay in the workers' village. I know some artisans who worked in my father's tomb. We can disguise ourselves between them.'

She sat half-turned, still looking at him. 'I've a favour to ask. Can we do one thing first?'

'What?'

'Visit the Temple of Sobek.' Before he could interrupt, she went on. 'Please, Tuthmosis. It's just around this bend in the river. I need to say farewell to my father's presence there. Perhaps all the rumours we received in Nubia were untrue. Maybe he's still alive.'

'Isikara, you don't truly believe this?'

'No, but I have to see the Temple for myself.'

Tuthmosis shook his head. 'It's too dangerous. We can't stop. What if we're spotted?'

'I *must*. Even if it's just to ask for the blessing of the Crocodile God, Sobek.'

'But we don't need the blessing of Sobek!'

She turned her back on him and began paddling again.

Tuthmosis slapped his paddle against the water. 'You're so stubborn! Stop if you must for a moment's glance and then let's be on our way.'

They paddled hard for the next while and when the tall, familiar columns of the Temple appeared ahead with the river lapping its wide, stone steps, they lifted their paddles and allowed the boat to drift forward in silence towards the wooden quay. Isikara could see that the walls of the Sacred Crocodile pool alongside the bank had been neglected. There were gaps and stones missing. Any crocodiles taken for ritual washing would have easily escaped into the river.

She clutched at her amulets and said a quick prayer. *Great Sobek, forgive me. I left your Temple because I had to escape Thebes. It's not my fault you've not been properly served.* Then she searched the water around their boat for a sign of bubbles that meant a crocodile might be lurking under the surface.

'Be careful, Tuthmosis,' she whispered. 'It looks as if no one has made offerings to Sobek for a long while. He's a fierce god. He could take revenge. A flick of his tail will overturn our boat. I know how fast crocodiles attack. Keep watch while I swing the boat towards the quay. Search the banks too.'

'We're *not* stopping. Pray quickly for a blessing from the boat and let's move on.'

'I *can't* just pass by. The Temple was my home.'

He frowned back at her. 'It's too dangerous, Isikara.'

'It'll be more dangerous if we don't stop. We *have* to show Sobek respect. I *was* a temple assistant here, after all.'

'Sobek's an old god. Of your father's times. Things have changed since then. You can see the Temple's not being used. No one is worrying about Sobek now.'

'Tuthmosis, trust me! We *have* to honour Sobek! I know it in my bones!' Isikara grabbed at some reeds and stood up as she drew the boat alongside the quay.

'No!' He wedged his paddle against the quay to try to push the boat back from it.

But she was already balancing with one foot over the side. She took a huge leap and landed on the quay while the boat was left wobbling. 'I'll be fine. The Temple's empty. You can see for yourself how neglected it is. It's a disgrace!'

'You don't know for sure!'

She tossed her head and stared back at him. His crystal blue eyes took on an opaque, smoky colour. She knew that look. 'Stay in the boat if you must. I'll go alone!' She turned and hurried along the rough wooden planks that were beginning to split and crack, towards the steps, and then glanced back quickly over her shoulder. 'I won't be long.'

'Don't be foolish, Isikara! You're risking everything with your stubbornness!' Tuthmosis's voice echoed hollowly against the stone columns with their decorations of lotus flowers and papyrus as she passed into the dark shadow of the Temple.

A breeze shivered through the reeds and rustled the papyrus heads back and forth. Some green-backed herons were nesting between the reeds and there were circles in the water as fish surfaced to gulp at flying insects. Two pied kingfishers hovered above, making sudden plummets as they dived for the fish.

Tuthmosis checked the height of the sun above the palm trees on the western bank. It was sinking fast.

It would be dark by the time they reached Thebes. It was risky to have stopped so close to the city. News might have reached Wosret that they were returning. Wosret would already know his army had been defeated in Nubia. He would also know he and Isikara were still free. What if this was a plot to capture them? A trap? Wosret might've guessed Isikara wouldn't be able to pass the Temple without stopping.

What was taking her so long in there? What if she was already held captive?

Tuthmosis secured the boat firmly and went up the stone steps after her.

The Temple was shadowy and smelt of wet earth and dampness. He paused to allow his eyes to get used to the gloom. Shafts of sunlight fell across the floor making the dark corners even darker. The river had clearly risen higher than the steps recently and flooded in. Black mud and debris lay scattered across the stone floor.

'Isikara!' he whispered urgently.

There was no knowing what was in the chambers ahead . . . who was lying in wait.

A breeze rustled some dry strands of reed at his feet. A bread offering, hard as stone, and some shrivelled lotus flowers lay strewn across an altar. On the wall above was a life-size carving of the crocodile-headed

Sobek standing upright, wearing a plumed headdress with a horned sun-disc. His eyes seemed to follow Tuthmosis as he crossed the room.

'*Isikara?*' he whispered into a darker chamber that led from the first courtyard. His voice echoed back hollowly. There was no sound of footsteps but the floor had marks in the dirt as if something heavy had been dragged across it. He peered down a dark stone stairwell. A few broken pottery jars lay discarded below. An imprint of a foot had dried hard in the layer of mud on the steps. Beyond that, he made out shapes that seemed to be small, mummified crocodiles wrapped in linen strips that were lined up like loaves on shelves around the walls, ready to be baked.

A noise made him spin around. Suddenly he was standing face to face with the largest crocodile he had ever seen.

It lay with its body half in shadow, wedged along a narrow stone shelf, its head raised in strike posture, its mouth agape and its teeth exposed – more frightening than any carving of Sobek.

He could smell the fetid, rotting-meat stench of its breath as it fixed him with eyes that glowed red in the half-gloom. As their eyes locked, he knew he would never live to tell his brother the truth. The chamber was too narrow for him to get safely past. There was no escape. A dash for the doorway wouldn't save him. The crocodile would be quicker.

He heard the hiss that came from the crocodile's mouth as its jaws dislocated in readiness for the lunge. Then, just as the head snapped forward, it seemed to choke in mid-air. From the corner of his eye, Tuthmosis caught a glimpse of Isikara as she thrust a forked branch at the crocodile's throat and pinned its head backwards against the stone wall. Its jaws were held clamped and its legs slithered as it tried to get a grip on the slimy stone shelf.

'Get around him! Quick! Come over to this side!' Isikara hissed. 'I won't be able to hold him pinned much longer.'

For a moment Tuthmosis was paralysed, his legs ready to slip out from under him, but then suddenly he managed to rush past the thrashing body.

He tried to grab the branch from Isikara.

'No! Get away!' she shouted. 'If I lose my grip now, he'll lunge at both of us. I know what I'm doing. As long as I can keep the jaws clamped shut, he's under control.'

'Kara, please . . .'

The crocodile was thrashing its huge tail but the confined space and the slippery stone surface were hampering it.

'Get a rock!' she shouted. 'I have to wedge the branch. Hurry! I can't hold it much longer!'

A rock? He heaved a stone off the broken wall and rolled it across the paving. Isikara's face was stricken with the effort of keeping the branch in place. For a moment it seemed too late. She was losing her grip. But then the rock was up against the wall and the branch wedged tightly behind it.

'Now run!' she shouted and, without stopping to check whether it held, they sprinted out through the Temple and down the steps to the boat.

Tuthmosis's hands trembled uncontrollably as he tried to loosen the rope that held the boat. Then suddenly they swung free out into the river, away from the bank and the Temple steps. As he looked back, he saw the crocodile was already slithering down the steps after them. At the quay it lifted its heavy body high on its legs and ran along the bank in a strange dog-like movement before plunging into the water. But they were far out in the main stream now, where the current was swifter. No matter how fast it swam, it wouldn't catch them.

They dug their paddles into the water, too shocked to speak. In front of him, he heard Isikara breathing hard. His own breath was still coming in short, jerky gasps.

Eventually Tuthmosis found his voice. 'If I have to meet a crocodile ever again, I want you at my side, Isikara. How did you know what to do?'

'It was luck. I found the forked branch my brother and I always used to control them in the crocodile pit.' Then she laughed. 'And perhaps my prayers to Sobek were answered very quickly.'

Ahead of them on the western bank, the sun was a ball of fire skimming just above the horizon, while on the eastern bank a full moon rose, huge and red as a split pomegranate, like a second sun in the sky.

They hung low on the horizon on either side of the wide river, glowing as red as a crocodile's eyes in the dusky light. The Eye of the Sun and the Eye of the Moon. The two wedjat eyes of Horus.

As they paddled towards them Isikara's smile was swept away by an overwhelming feeling of dread. The two burning discs seemed like a warning of what was still to come. Who knew what lay ahead in Thebes?

CHAPTER THIRTEEN

THE PLACE OF MAAT

It was dark by the time Tuthmosis and Isikara arrived at the quayside on the western bank of Thebes. The men who hired out donkeys had all gone home for the night and the moon was already small and remote in the sky as they walked the dusty road towards the Place of Maat. Even the stars seemed remote and indifferent. Isikara cursed herself for being so head-strong. She knew what Tuthmosis was thinking. If she hadn't been so insistent on stopping at the Temple of Sobek, they would have been safely asleep in the village by now instead of dragging their feet through the dust in the middle of the night.

Tuthmosis must have sensed her thoughts because he turned and smiled. 'We've come at the best time.

Everyone is already asleep. No one will see us.'

In the moonlight ahead she caught sight of a silvery jackal. It stopped for a brief second to stare at them and went hurriedly on. Then, just as suddenly, where the road took a bend around some boulders she saw small lights bobbing ahead of them.

Tuthmosis pulled her down. 'Quick! Get behind the boulders. They're coming this way.'

Her heart beat high up in her throat. 'Who?'

Tuthmosis shrugged. 'Soldiers perhaps.'

She saw him finger the hilt of a dagger hidden beneath the folds of his tunic.

'Soldiers? Out in the middle of the night?'

'On patrol perhaps.'

'Looking for us? How would anyone know we've returned?'

'Wosret has spies. They could've seen us on the river.'

Isikara gripped hold of his arm. This was worse than the moment in the desert when the Medjay raiders had come after them on camels. At least they'd been well-hidden then. But now only a few boulders lay between them and the path along which the men were coming. It *had* to be a search party. Why else were they carrying lamps and why were there so many of them?

And now Isikara caught the coppery glint of weapons, slung across their shoulders and hanging from their girdles. And as they drew closer she felt the heavy tramp of their feet in the earth beneath her sandals.

'What'll we do?' she hissed.

'Get your dagger ready.'

Her heart seemed to stop. Her dagger? She hadn't used a dagger since that night in the Medjay camp. And even now the thought of the dark blood seeping through the man's tunic and staining her hands turned her to stone. No! *No!* She couldn't use a dagger again. Not ever. Not even to defend her life!

Tuthmosis must have seen her hesitate. 'You have to, Isikara. Grab your dagger! We can't be captured so close to our journey's end.'

'I can't!' She could hear the hoarseness in her voice. 'I can't do this, Tuthmosis! Not again!'

She felt his hand grip her arm. 'You *must!*'

As he spoke, the group of men drew level with the boulders and then suddenly they veered away on another path she hadn't noticed.

She felt her body go slack and all the breath leave her.

In the moonlight Tuthmosis was grinning. 'Did you see? They were workers. Not *soldiers*. They were

127

carrying implements and chisels for hacking rock, not people! They're stone-cutters.'

'Stone-cutters?'

He nodded. 'Going off to work in the royal tombs.'

'At this time of night?'

'The tombs are dark. They work shifts all through the night. What does it matter whether it's day or night when you work by lamplight deep inside a mountain?'

He led her back onto the deserted road where moments ago the men had tramped. They passed the village well and went through the north gate into the silent village lit only here and there by a lamp. Dark, narrow alleyways led away from the single main road. But Tuthmosis seemed sure of his way. He led them to a mud-brick house and tapped lightly on the door that had a rough, mud-sculpted cobra above the lintel. A dog started to howl and Tuthmosis picked up a clod of earth and threw it at him. Then a muffled voice called out, 'Yes . . .? Who is it?'

'Tut.'

Tut? Isikara glanced quickly at his face. Is this what his friends called him?

'What? It can't be!' The door opened a crack and a huge, tousled-looking young man peered out through the gap. He clutched a weapon close to his body.

128

'It's truly me, Hera. Quick, let us in!'

The door swung back. 'By Horus, where have you come from, Tut?' He enfolded Tuthmosis in a lion hug. 'What are you doing here? I heard you were lost somewhere in Nubia. And who . . .' his eyes swept to Isikara, '. . . is this?'

'She's a friend.'

'*She?*' He gave Isikara another swift glance. 'I thought her a *boy*!'

'Shh! Don't speak so loudly. Your neighbours will hear. Isikara's in disguise. She's the daughter of the embalmer, Henuka. Quick! Shut the door! We need to be hidden. Just for a few days until I get a message through to my brother.'

Hera turned and fumbled with a lamp that was finally lit and the small room took on a glow. 'I thought you were at war in Nubia but here you are! Have you come to claim your throne back from Amenhotep?'

Tuthmosis shook his head.

Hera raised an eyebrow. 'If not to claim the throne, then what?'

'I must warn Amenhotep of Wosret.'

'You must clear your name of scandal too. There are all sorts of rumours. They say you took up arms against Egypt.'

Tuthmosis nodded. 'I need to know what's been said, but first I want to confront Wosret and get him to admit he tried to poison me and planned my death so my brother could be King.'

Hera shook his head. 'Wosret will *never* admit. He has too much to lose. He wanted a young King he could control. He seems to be taming Nefertiti as well.'

'That's all the more reason to meet with Amenhotep quickly. Will you hide us?'

Hera gave Isikara a quick look. '*Both* of you? This is a household of workmen. I've seven brothers. We'll be too rough for her.'

Isikara tossed her head. 'I'm used to men. I've fought in the Nubian army. Besides, I've a brother. I'll cope.'

'You'd be better off with a woman. There's not much space here. It's easier to hide one person rather than two. When we go off to work or sleep in shifts, the village is full of wives and children. I've an aunt you can stay with. She travels to Thebes often. She works there as a chantress. You'll be safe with her.'

Isikara looked across at Tuthmosis. 'I . . .'

'Hera's right. It'll be safer if we split up.'

'But . . .'

'It's only until I speak to my brother. Once he's on our side, we won't have to hide.'

'We've been together since . . .' Her voice faltered and she felt the warmth rising in her cheeks.

Hera laughed as he looked between them then he gave Tuthmosis another huge lion hug. 'You've fallen in love, Tut. I can see it! Come! Let's make plans before the dawn shift of workmen wakes up. The one we must dodge is the new Vizier of the village. A fierce fellow by the name of Ramose.'

'What happened to the last Vizier?'

'Wosret got rid of him. Said he was too lenient and taking bribes. Which wasn't true but it suited Wosret to have someone here he could control. The new Vizier sits as Chief Magistrate of the local court here in the village. And he in turn has appointed a whole phalanx of foremen who are responsible for over-seeing the removal of tools from the royal storehouse and scribes who distribute our food-wages and make note of workmen who are dodging work. There are always squabbles about irregular deliveries of fish, and beer, and wood for fuel, and grain. But if you play your game right and work hard, extra luxuries are provided, like salt and sesame oil. But I warn you, the new Vizier is a tough one to handle and has spies everywhere. So we'll have to be sharp. And pray to the Cobra Goddess who lives at the top of our mountain to protect us.'

CHAPTER FOURTEEN

THE PRISON – KIYA

'Are you there? Wake up now. You've been sleeping all morning. I heard someone asking for you. Listen now. Is that your boyfriend's voice? He's asking the guards whether he can see you and they're putting up a fuss.'

It wasn't Samut's voice. It was Kiya's. I felt a flare of hope. Yet when I looked up it wasn't Kiya standing in front of me at the gate, but some urchin boy with a short, rough wig and a ragged, coarse tunic that covered his chest and a girdle and leather bag about his waist. His face was smeared with dirt.

'What do you want with me?' I snarled out of desperation at this rough urchin and sank back onto the stone floor.

'Ta-Miu, it's me.'

'*Kiya?*' I looked up again. 'Is that truly you?'

'Shh! Don't say my name so loudly. Can't you see I'm disguised as a boy?' She grinned back at me and then reached through the bars. 'Ta-Miu, you look awful. Don't they feed you? Don't you wash?'

I gripped the gate. 'Get me out of here!'

'And your hands are bleeding. What have you done to them?'

'Her hands bleed because she scratches at the wall. Words, she says. All day long. Scratch, scratch, scratch. And doesn't eat. Not that I mind. The guards give her food to me. Can't let it go to waste! Pig's swill, that's what it is. But a person has to eat. Come here! Let me look at you. You're not Samut, are you? No, I don't imagine you are. Too young to be Samut. Cheeks too smooth. Hands too dainty and voice not yet broken in. Stand a little closer to my gate so I can see you. You wouldn't be a girl, would you?'

'I'll keep my distance, thank you. And no, I'm not a girl.'

I shook my head and whispered to Kiya. 'Take no notice of her. She's been here seven years. She listens in to everything I do. I can't move without her saying something.'

Kiya turned to the woman. 'I'll ask you not to listen

while I speak to my sister. If I share some of the food
I brought, will you keep away and busy yourself in the
back of your cell?'

'Your *sister*? Hmm. She said nothing of a brother.
Why haven't you come before now?'

'I don't have to explain to you. And I *am* her
brother!'

'A cheeky boy at that! With lots to say for himself.
Give me the food, then. If it's worth it, I'll stay away.'

'Give it all to her, Kiya. She can have my share.
I'm not hungry.'

'No. You must eat, Ta-Miu. I've brought smoked
duck and peacock hearts and honey cakes and grapes
for their sweetness.'

'Smoked duck and peacock hearts! By the feather of
Maat, can it be true? A piece of smoked duck hasn't
passed my lips for more than seven years. And as for
peacock heart! Well I never! Such delicacies for the
likes of her . . . a thief!'

'You won't even *smell* any of the peacock heart. It's
all hers. My sister needs the strength! Here! Take these
slices of duck and these cakes and grapes and be
silent.'

'Hmm! Strong words from a mere boy. Where
are your manners? Did your mother not teach you
to respect your elders? Where have you learnt such

imperious ways? Are you sure you're just a peasant boy? Come closer to the front of my gate so I can see you. My eyes have grown dim in here.'

'If you want the food take it now, or the offer no longer stands.'

'You don't fool me. You're not who you say you are! Doesn't help though, does it? Being grand and yet having no one to save you! Very well, I'll take it and sit in a corner and do as I'm told. I've got used to taking orders these seven years.'

Kiya turned to me. 'At last! Hurry, Ta-Miu, eat while I tell you the news. Tuthmosis is back!'

'*Tuthmosis!* What? Who told you?'

'They say he's here in Thebes and that girl is with him.'

'The girl? You mean, Isikara? The girl he escaped with?'

'Yes, the daughter of the embalmer at the Temple of the Crocodile God, Sobek.'

'Why have they returned?'

'No one knows, but the Palace is in turmoil. There are guards everywhere. That's why I couldn't come before.'

'And what about Samut? Why hasn't *he* come?'

Kiya pulled at a loose strand of her boy wig. 'No one has seen Samut for days. I've asked my serving girls for news of him. They say he's disappeared.'

I reached through the bars and grabbed hold of her arm. 'He *can't* have. If he's left Thebes how will I be freed? Who will speak out for me?'

'Ta-Miu, you must believe me, Samut's not to be trusted. He's the tomb robber. The ring is proof of that. But he's happy for Tuthmosis and you to take the blame. If that's what Wosret believes, why should he confess?'

'But what about *me*? I'm completely innocent. Surely he'll confess to giving me the ring?'

Kiya's silence told me she had doubts.

'Do *you* believe I'm innocent?'

She twitched her shoulders. 'Of course I do, but others don't.'

'Samut *must* speak up for me.'

'And ruin his life? Why should he do that?'

'Because he said he loved me.'

Kiya stared back at me.

I stamped my foot. '*What?* What are you looking at?'

She kept silent.

'Then *why* did he give me the ring?'

'Ta-Miu, forget about protecting Samut. He's deserted you. You have to speak out against him. It's your only chance to free yourself.' Kiya stared back

137

at me silently through the bars and then nodded. 'You have to, Ta-Miu. You have to confess he was the tomb robber.'

'Not until he tells me so himself.'

'Then you'll *never* leave here.' She put her hand through the bars and touched my shoulder. 'We both fell for his charm.'

Our eyes met. It was strange that she was now my comforter. That our roles had been reversed. 'Can't you plead my case with Amenhotep?'

She shook her head. 'I haven't had the opportunity. Thebes has been in an uproar since the news of Tuthmosis came out. Secrets and rumours are rife. Nefertiti is anxious. She knows whatever happens the throne might be taken from Amenhotep. She'll lose her position. She won't stand for this!'

'So what's to be done about me?'

'Can't you see? You know the truth. You know Tuthmosis didn't rob his father's tomb. You know he left Thebes without a single jewel. You were the only one who saw him leave that night . . . you and Isikara. You helped them both escape while everyone was at the Temple celebrating the rebirth of the star, Sophet, and the rising of the Great River.'

'It's true.'

'Then speak out, Ta-Miu. Tell the truth. Denounce

Samut. Tell Wosret that Samut was the tomb robber. Clear yourself.'

I stepped back from the gate beyond her reach. 'You make it sound so easy. But I cannot! Tomb robbers are put to death.' I blocked my ears. 'Stop this, Kiya! I can't speak out against Samut!'

No, I couldn't. I had lain in his arms. We'd whispered stories to each other. He'd kept his face so close to mine, I'd had to shut my eyes to steady myself. He'd taken my cheeks in his hands and dropped kisses on my eyelids. He had said he was a tomb robber. But he'd been joking. It couldn't be true. And yet . . .? No! He couldn't have done something so dreadful. Of *course* he was joking.

I would *never* speak out against Samut. Never!

CHAPTER FIFTEEN

WOSRET

The full face of the Moon-God, Khonsu, had already dipped towards the west and was losing its brightness in a layer of smoky dust that clung to the horizon.

Wosret's skin felt sticky with sweat. The night was sultry and the streets of Thebes were empty and dark. A hot night wind blowing in from the desert brought with it a fine haze of dust that dulled the stars, making the night even murkier. A fine layer of grit had settled on him.

A rat scuttling out suddenly from beneath a bundle of reeds startled him, but otherwise the street was silent and empty, except for the dry rattle of palm leaves and the rasp of stray pieces of reed scraping against the dirt as they blew down the road.

Even the alleyways were silent except for a single dog that nosed around some discarded bones, cracking them under his teeth. The sound echoed in the silence. Every now and again the dog stood with his head alert as if expecting a stray hyena or desert jackal to slink into his territory. As Wosret approached the dog loped off towards the outskirts of the town where the mud houses and alleyways gave way to the desert, marking his territory all the way as he ran off to sniff out an unwary rat. In the darkness his outline soon blurred against the sand.

Wosret followed up the empty street, but turned between the shadows of the sphinxes towards the new Southern Opet Temple. He'd chosen the Temple because if someone were to enter by chance, they'd not be unduly surprised to find a priest there. Yet still he'd taken the precaution of covering his shaven head and priestly garments with a cloak.

His stomach grumbled. The hour was late and the leg of tasty venison he'd dined on and the goblets of good wine he'd drunk had long been digested. The kitchen fires had died down and there was nothing to be had out on the empty streets at this late hour. If only he had had a third helping of that succulent antelope.

He passed through the huge pylon gates with their

mammoth cedar posts and flapping pennants and the towering statue of the old King. The eyes stared blankly past him across the gilded paving and over the gardens that were still being laid out, all the way down towards the banks of the Great River where the moon hovered.

He entered the gilded colonnade with its pairs of papyrus-shaped columns and searched the shadows for a sign of the person he was supposed to meet. But the paving rung only with the sound of his own feet.

There was a smell of dust and damp pigment in the air. Carvings and inscriptions along the walls were still being worked and scenes were still being painted. King Amenhotep had hoped to have them completed in his reign but his death had been sudden. Now it was his job to see they were finished according to what the King had prescribed. King Amenhotep leading military expeditions in his chariot. King Amenhotep conquering his enemies. King Amenhotep receiving gifts of gold and ivory from his dominions.

And now of course the new, *young* Amenhotep would want to be included as well, even though he had barely begun to shave! And then there was Nefertiti! She would require an *entire wall* of carvings devoted wholly to her. Yes, she showed all the signs of being a feisty, determined and *very* demanding young woman.

His work would be cut out for him trying to direct her the way he wished her to go! She was as strong-willed as a camel that had just smelt water and was dead set on reaching it.

As he scrutinised the new carvings in the dim light, he scowled. Could it be? Was that *small* figure carrying Amun's Barque a depiction of himself? Was this how he was to be seen by the world? He frowned up at the figure of King Amenhotep who strode beside him like a colossus. He would need to remind the carvers to enlarge his own figure. It was true a King should tower over all his subjects and his enemies, but there was no need for the Highest of High Priests to *cower* beneath the armpits of a King! It looked ridiculous! No, he must definitely remember to speak to the carvers. A little bit of height was needed to add stature.

At the end of the colonnade he bowed before the seated statues of the god Amun and his wife, Mut. It had been his idea to install all three of the Theban triad – not just Amun and Mut but also their son Khonsu – in the new Temple.

He hurried beyond the colonnade into the vast paved Great Sun Court of King Amenhotep and swept his eyes impatiently around the open space. Where was this fellow he was supposed to be meeting at this late hour? He began to regret his decision to come. The message had been secretly delivered. Pushed under his door in the middle of the night. The person hadn't left his name. He'd merely said he had a secret to exchange – important news – and asked to meet in a place and at a time when they would not be seen.

The Great Sun Court was a place where commoners were permitted to enter to celebrate special festivals and to allow them closer access to the gods. But no one would be about now. To impress the commoners King Amenhotep had ordered scenes showing people paying homage to their great Pharaoh at the time of the Opet Festival, when Amun's golden statue was carried between the two Temples of Thebes. Wosret nodded. Yes, this was the way it should be. Amun would be celebrated in the darkest recess of the Most Holy of Holy Places in the Inner Sanctum where only *he*, Wosret, the King and a few selected priests could enter, away from the eyes of the common people.

But now he was impatient with all this. He wanted his bed or some food at least. But the daily offering tables had been cleared by the priests. There was not a scrap left to be eaten, and even if a loaf of bread had been forgotten, the mice would've demolished it by now. A few lone strands of lotus flowers lay limply against the stone altar, giving off a heady perfume.

Where *was* this fellow? Why was he being so tardy? Didn't he know that one didn't keep the Highest of High Priests waiting?

He passed into the utter darkness of the hypostyle hall with its tall rows of columns that held up the solid stone slabs spanning the roof. Not a vestige of Khonsu's moonlight entered here. On the far side, in some niches next to the small chambers dedicated to Mut and Khonsu, two oil lamps were burning. He removed one and entered a small chamber to the west. The Moon-God Khonsu stood tall and upright in the flickering light with the full moon-disc resting in the cup of a crescent moon on his head and a sickle-shaped moon pectoral across his chest. His sacred baboon was at his feet and in his hands he held the crook and flail of Horus.

Wosret bowed. He might as well use his time to gain favour. An extra prayer might reap rewards.

I built this house for thee, Khonsu, God of Rebirth, God of the Moon, and overlaid its doorposts and doors with gold, to look like the horizon of Heaven. I have decorated the walls with your image being carried on your sacred Barque with its falcon's head at the prow on your special festival when the Birth of the New Year is celebrated. Look

*down now on your humble servant and grant my request
that Nefertiti will soon give birth.*

It was right to make the request now. In a few more
nights Khonsu would turn his face away and then
the new moon would hang thin as a nail paring in the
sky. Everyone knew the time of the New Moon was
the time of rebirth, when Khonsu allowed women
to conceive.

A baby son would keep Nefertiti occupied and
less troublesome so he, Wosret, could get on with the
job of governing Egypt the way *he* saw fit.

An echo of footsteps made him turn. In the
doorway of the chamber stood a figure with a cloak
pulled across his face.

Wosret narrowed his eyes. 'What's your name,
fellow?'

'The information I give, sir, has no need of a name.'

Wosret glanced beyond the man into the shadows.
'How can I be sure you weren't followed?'

'I'm no stranger to the need for vigilance.'

'Drop your cloak then so I can see you're unarmed.'

As he did so, Wosret scrutinised him, trying to
recall where he had seen this face before. 'Do I know
you? Have we not met before?'

The young man shook his head. 'I don't think we
frequent the same places.'

Wosret studied him carefully. 'How can you presume I want this information from you?'

The young man held his look. 'You wouldn't be here otherwise.'

Wosret sighed heavily. 'Well, let's get on with it, then, but not under the eyes of Khonsu. Pass through the doorway into the portico and the room ahead. In that room is the Barque of Amun. You must swear on the holy Barque that you speak the truth.'

Wosret held the lamp high to light the way. The young man's shoulders were broad and muscled and he had the confident air of someone not used to being subservient.

They stood in the small stuffy chamber that enclosed Amun's Barque. Wosret nodded. 'Get on with it, then. What do you want to tell me? And, more importantly, what favour do you need of me?'

In the lamplight, Wosret saw the young man arch an eyebrow. 'I've no favour to ask, but a man never knows when one is needed.'

'That's true. Place a hand on Amun's Sacred Barque then, and say what you have to say. I'm in a hurry to be home.'

'Tuthmosis has returned to Thebes. He has come to claim his Kingship back from his brother.'

Wosret gave him a dark look. 'Is that *all* you have

to say? You kept me from my bed to tell me *this*! Why do you think I've so many guards on duty?'

'You don't know Tuthmosis's exact whereabouts and intentions. I do.'

'How can you? Do you have some magical powers? Are you a mind-reader?'

The man shook his head. 'He's disguised.'

'Then how do you know it's truly him?'

'I know his face and those blue eyes. He's in the Place of Maat. The girl, Isikara, the one he escaped with, is there as well. They're staying in different places but I know the exact houses where they're hiding.'

CHAPTER SIXTEEN

THE PRISON – TA-MIU

Treachery is difficult to live with. It's a viper that rises up unexpectedly from the desert sands and strikes when you least expect it. The spells of the Afterlife invoke the heart not to be treacherous. Treachery covers both disloyalty and betrayal.

How am I to come to terms with Samut's disloyalty? Why has he deserted me? The thought of it catches me by my throat and paralyses me. I have been so foolish – but he said he loved me.

Betrayal is an even worse form of treachery. Yet who was more treacherous? I, for betraying the secret of the duplicate key? Or Samut, for acting on it?

*

'He no longer loves you!'

Did I say the words out aloud? My mind is muddled. Since Kiya's visit I've been over and over what she said but nothing is clear. I'm tired. I need sleep.

'The boy you spoke of no longer loves you. And that other boy wasn't your brother, was he?'

It is the old woman speaking. I keep my lips shut tight. Why does she want so many answers?

'Don't feel like speaking again today? Well, see if I'm bothered. The smoked duck wasn't as tasty as it should've been. Dried out and overcooked, I'd say. Don't think I'll be bowing and scraping to you just because you think you're important enough to have smoked duck and peacock hearts brought to you. And not even a drop of wine to wash it down with!'

I gripped the ankh and began gouging at the walls again.

Samut shows me the Palace chariot house and the stables with their stone water basins and their sloping floors and troughs at the lower end for keeping the floor as dry as possible and for catching the horses' urine. We go on a night when the Moon-God, Khonsu, is showing just a slither of his face. Our path through the Palace gardens is dark and silent. We time the guards' movements and wait for the stable boy to leave.

What noise the horses make when they hear Samut's voice! He calls them with sounds through his teeth and speaks in low murmurs that aren't proper words. They answer with snorts and whinnies and stamps of their hooves. I worry the noise will bring the guards running and wake everyone in the Palace. Samut goes up and down the stalls talking to each one, rubbing across the bridges of their noses, blowing into their faces and stroking their flanks while the horses nuzzle his neck and toss their heads and arch their swan necks and try to push their way out of each stall to get closer to him even though they are tethered.

He has the same manner with horses as the horsemen who brought Kiya and me to Egypt from Mitanni. But even those horsemen never received as much attention from their horses as these ones give Samut.

They're not war horses. They're hunting horses, he tells me, *trained to chase across the desert weaving back and forth after the swiftest antelope or cheetah, pulling marksmen in chariots behind them.*

I nod. I know but stay silent. In Mitanni we called

151

them Wind-eaters. Horses that run swifter than the wind. Running fast enough to swallow it.

King Amenhotep's two favourite stallions are here still. Come and see, he says and takes my hand.

I gaze at Maarqada, a horse as black as the night, with fearless eyes, and Mimreh, a dark bay with a proud strong neck.

They wore duplicates of King Amenhotep's chest pectorals and the leopard cloak of honour across their backs when they pulled his chariot. Now Amenhotep the son has claimed them and Nefertiti too has been given a pair of chestnut stallions for her own chariot.

He spreads his hands for me to see. *This is where my scars come from. I worked here as a boy.*

So he is not a falconer. Nor is he a tomb robber. That's why he's brought me here. That's why he knows so much about the horses and why he knew how to bind my leg. He'd bound sprained ankles . . . or rather sprained fetlocks before.

My father was Chief Vizier of the stables. King Amenhotep sent envoys to your country to find the very best horse-trainer to make sure his horses were the fastest, strongest and finest-bred horses ever seen. The trainer worked them until he knew the precise moment when each horse was both physically and instinctively ready for what lay ahead. He wasn't going to risk his own life by having the King thrown out of his chariot because of a badly-trained horse!

Samut was telling me these things. But I knew them of course. I was from the Khabur mountains. We were horsemen. My father's father and his father before him and my brothers. It was in my blood.

The trainer used unusual methods. Instead of putting them behind a chariot, he made them trot and canter over exactly marked distances for long periods until their muscles were strong and lean. He identified horses with breathing problems by blocking all the cracks in the stable walls to increase dust and mould. Any horse with the slightest chest problem was rejected.

All this Samut reports as we pass through the stables, stall by stall. He interrupts himself to pause and murmur to each individual horse. I say nothing but walk with my hand twined in his. We come to the room where the chariots and harnesses and fodder are stored. A strong smell of leather and straw and newly-shaved wood hangs in the air.

Sit here with me here, Ta-Miu, he says.

A stray stable cat comes and purrs up against us. And Samut traces lightly over the cat tattoo on my shoulder. I feel his breath against my neck. We lie down with the straw as our pillow. I lie in his arms so close that I see myself reflected in his eyes. He touches

153

the two cords about my neck and holds the glass
scarab and ankh in turn. Then he raises my chin and
kisses me on the mouth. His skin smells of straw and
leather and the sweet-sour smell of horses and his
mouth tastes of honey. Something like a fire burns
through my body. I want to melt in his arms as his
lips touch mine.

Whose heart does the ankh open? He whispers next
to my ear.

I shake my head dreamily. *It's just a key.*

Just a key . . . ?

I press my fingers against his lips.

But what key? A key to what?

If I tell you, will you never speak of it again?

He nods. *I promise.*

*It's a key to a gate that guards the secret entry from the
Palace gardens into the King's labyrinth and his burial
chambers.*

King Amenhotep's burial chambers?

I nod and see my face reflected in Samut's eyes.

And then I tell him about the other key. The
duplicate one that is hidden on a shelf just within the
gate.

So who is the more treacherous now? Samut, or I?

CHAPTER SEVENTEEN

THE PLACE OF MAAT

The silence of the room was broken by the scratch of Tuthmosis's stylus against papyrus.

Outside in the street children were making up rhyming games and some boys were batting a ball with a stick and shouting at their smaller brothers to catch. The walls were papyrus thin. He could hear someone in the next-door house scolding a child for allowing the dog inside. A sound of chopping and an aroma of chickpeas and onions and smells of roasted pigeon came drifting to him from the outer room where Hera's mother was preparing the evening meal.

In a niche above him, a statue of the impish household god, Bes, was dancing to the bang of his cymbals, frightening away the evil spells. By the slant of sunshine entering the high, west window at the top of the room, Tuthmosis knew it was almost time for the workers to come back from their day shift. Hera was right. The village was like a skeleton during the day, that lost all its flesh and muscle and brawn. Soon the front door would be flung open and he'd have to hide in the hot, stuffy cellar again while Hera's boisterous brothers ate supper and drank their daily ration of beer with their neighbours. Not until the village settled down for sleep would he be able to come out and lie with the family on mats on the open roof under the stars, with the side walls screening him from inquisitive neighbours.

He was anxious to get the message to his brother. Every now and again the point of his stylus caught against an uneven bump of papyrus and sent a spray of sooty ink over the surface. Eventually the final stroke was drawn and all that had to be said, was said. Amenhotep would *have* to believe him. Hera had promised it would be delivered into the King's own hands. He blew hurriedly across the surface to dry the ink before he rolled the papyrus and dropped a blob of warm wax across the edge. Then he turned his ring and pressed its seal into the wax. Hera would make sure the seal wasn't broken by the wrong person.

He had warned Hera the night before. 'The letter

156

will contain every detail of Wosret's plot to take over Egypt and all he has done to wrong me. If Wosret gets hold of it before my brother, I won't stand a chance. My throat will be slit before I can prove myself.'

Hera had given his word. 'I'll give it to one of the King's bedchamber attendants. I've been painting the wings of the Vulture Goddess across the ceiling in his chamber. Your brother often comes to inspect the work. Perhaps I'll even see him break the seal.'

'Whatever happens, you *must* be vigilant. My life's at stake. Wosret has tried to poison me before. He won't allow his plans to be stopped again. He wants me out of the way.'

'By my breath, trust me! How long have you known me, Tut? I'll make sure the letter is given secretly into the right hands. I won't forget that when I was only an apprentice mixing pigments in your father's tomb, you had me promoted. You have my word, Tut, I won't fail you.'

Now, as Tuthmosis withdrew his sealing ring from the wax on the papyrus, he heard angry shouts coming from outside and Hera's rather large mother came rushing from the back room and heaved herself breathlessly up the steps to the open rooftop.

'Come quickly!' she panted as she passed him. 'But don't allow yourself to be seen.'

They crouched below the low wall that rimmed the rooftop and peered down into the roadway below. Some men were banging on the door of a house a few paces away. It was the house Isikara was staying in. And before Tuthmosis could do anything, she was already being dragged out through the doorway into the road.

'Leave me be! I work in this village,' she shouted as she fought and kicked at them.

'Then show us your papers that say you are registered here.'

'Papers? Hah! And who amongst you brutes can even read?'

Tuthmosis clenched his fists. *Don't, Isikara! Don't make it worse for yourself! Just keep silent!*

'She was led into a trap!' Hera's mother whispered. 'Listen to what the women down there are saying. A child knocked on her door and said she was ill and needed water.'

'But where was your sister? Why didn't she answer the door?'

'It's her day for Temple duty. She's gone to Thebes.'

The men had tied Isikara's hands behind her back and were hoisting her onto a donkey. Tuthmosis slammed his fist into the palm of his hand. 'I can't just stand by and watch this. They're a bunch of brutes. What'll they do to her? I must go to her.'

'Are you stupid?' Hera's mother grabbed him by the shoulder and yanked him back. 'There'd be no point. How can you help? You'd just get arrested yourself.' Her chest heaved as she pushed him down below the wall again.

Tuthmosis tried to shrug her off. 'I have to! I can't leave her to these thugs.'

She puffed herself up to even larger proportions. 'Listen to me! Six soldiers against *one*? What madness! Even *I* wouldn't consider attacking them! Wait for my sons to return. They'll be here soon. They'll get her back before those soldiers have time to say Good Horus protect us! Trust me.'

'But who betrayed her? Your sister?'

'My *sister*?' Hera's mother glared at him, as if she wanted to give him a good clout across the head. 'The blood that runs through our family is as true and pure as any that runs through royalty. My sister's a proud, loyal person. She'd never break a promise and would *never* reveal the whereabouts of someone we promised to hide.'

'Who then? Who gave her away?'

She pointed. 'That hyena skulking over there. You can be sure. Doesn't do a day's work yet always has enough food and beer. If there's work to be done, don't look to him, but if there's beer to be had, then ...! I should've sued him the day he sold me that defective donkey for a pot of fat. I hope the fat went rancid on him. He has a hand in all sorts of deals and bribes and if I had a daughter I'd keep her locked up rather than have him around her!'

Tuthmosis peered out into the roadway to where Hera's mother was pointing. His breath caught. Of all the people who could have been standing there ... of all the people who could have given Isikara's hiding place away ... the water-carriers, the potters, the stonemasons, the chariot makers or any other of the workmen from the Place of Maat ... it was the one person he *least* expected.

One whom he hadn't seen since his childhood.

But *why* had he betrayed Isikara?

And now as Tuthmosis looked down, he saw him exchange glances with one of the soldiers and then turn and look deliberately at the house of Hera's family and give a small but definite nod.

'Quick! You have to make a run for it!' Hera's mother hissed. 'Go out through the kitchen into the alleyway and enter the third door on your left. It's my cousin's house. Hide there until all is quiet again. Hurry!'

CHAPTER EIGHTEEN

THE PRISON – ISIKARA

A noise woke me from a dream. I'd been dreaming of peacocks and a place high up between the mountains. Mountains with icy streams. There were horsemen, hundreds of them, and a woman tugging at me. But then my dream evaporated and I heard a noise coming from somewhere. Shouting and cursing and feet scuffling along the stone passage.

A girl's voice shouted out. 'You have no right to lock me up! I demand to speak to someone in authority. Who has given the order to take me prisoner? Let go of me!' she raged.

'Ouch! You bit me, you little vixen! A pestilence of flies on you, girl! May you rot here until your heart is scattered in the Field of Reeds!' There was the sound of a blow. A flat hand hitting against flesh.

'Do you have *no* feelings? What if I were your sister?'

'If you *were* my sister, I'd have you beaten for behaving like a vixen.'

'You dog! If you were my *brother* I'd pray your heart would be carried off by Ammut, Devourer of the Dead, to the Lake of Fire! Your heart is *already* dead!'

'And yours will be too! Get into that cell with this other wretched girl who puts on airs and graces far beyond her status.'

'Take your hands off me! I'm no wretched girl! I am Isikara, daughter of the Priest at the Temple of the Crocodile God, Sobek.'

Isikara? I pushed myself up hurriedly from my sleeping pallet. Could it really be her?

'Not any more!' the guard sneered. 'We all know what happened to your father. He was a traitor and got what traitors deserve. And you are no less a traitor.'

'Get away from me! May Sobek crunch your bones between his teeth and the wind scatter their grit over the desert!'

'You've no power to invoke Sobek!'

'Ha! You forget I was my father's helper at the Temple of Sobek. Who do you think fed, watered

162

and bathed the sacred crocodiles before the Festival of Opet and helped with their embalming? I've *all* the power in the Kingdom to invoke Sobek!'

'Wretched girl! You deserve worse than this cell. If you were my sister I'd have you not just beaten but put to *death*! A mouth as vicious as yours needs to be silenced.' The guard shoved her into the cell and banged the gate shut, jammed the bolt across and snapped the lock.

She sprawled against the floor, blood seeping from a cut on her cheek, her tunic ripped and filthy. She leapt up and grabbed hold of the bars and spat through them. 'And if you were my brother, I'd push you into the crocodile enclosure! You deserve no better than to be eaten by a crocodile,' she shouted after the echoing footsteps.

'A fine performance, deary!' the old woman from next door cackled. 'But it won't get you far. In fact you might rue the day you were so fiery. They like feisty girls but not fiery ones. The best is got from them by playing the girlish role. Flirting a little and playing up to their fragile egos.'

'I don't care about fragile egos. The girlish role no longer suits me! I've fought side by side with the Nubians. I know about war and battles.'

I peered at her. 'Isikara? Is that really you?'

'Yes, it's me. Who are *you?*' Her eyes raked across me.

'Don't you remember me? It's Ta-Miu. I helped you and Tuthmosis escape from the Palace. So it's true, then. You've returned. But what's happened? Where's Tuthmosis? Is he safe?'

Her eyes still flared with tiny stars of anger. 'They captured me. I don't know what happened to him.'

'You've changed, Isikara. I hardly recognised you.'

She wiped the blood on her cheek with the back of her hand. 'It's me, all the same. Days spent in a Medjay camp and training with a bow in the sun alongside Nubian bowmen would change anyone. You don't exactly look the same either.'

'I've been in prison a long time. I'm not sure how long.'

'Only seven *days*, deary! I've marked it off. You still have a long way to go to catch up with my seven *years!*'

Isikara's eyebrows shot up. She inclined her head towards the cell next door. 'Does she always listen in?'

I nodded.

She glared around the cramped space and gave an impatient twitch of her shoulders. 'I have to make plans. I must get out of here as quickly as possible.'

I eyed her. 'Do you think I haven't been trying? It's impossible.'

164

'Wosret has convinced everyone we're both traitors. That we helped Tuthmosis get away. He's also convinced them it was Tuthmosis who raided his father's tomb for its riches, before he escaped to Nubia to raise an army against Egypt.'

'I know, but it's not true.'

'We both know the truth. You must speak out. For all I know they might have captured Tuthmosis as well by now.'

'Speak out?' I glanced at her. How much did Isikara know?

She nodded. 'In the Place of Maat they say a boy gave you the ring.'

I twisted a piece of my tunic between my fingers. 'What if he did? It was only a copy of the real ring.'

She shook her head.

I gave her a hard look. 'Are you saying I'm a liar?'

'The jeweller who made the ring lives in the Place of Maat. He was arrested and asked to examine it and swore it was King Amenhotep's original ring. There's no other like it and it has the jeweller's mark stamped into the gold. Since the original is missing from the King's tomb, no further evidence is needed. The ring you were given is the real one that belonged to the King and was part of his wealth for the Afterlife.'

'May a frog lodge in your throat! That ring *wasn't* the real one.'

'You know I speak the truth. You *have* to tell Wosret who gave it to you.'

'I don't have to tell Wosret anything! And I don't have to listen to you! Why should I speak out?'

'A confession is our only chance of getting out of here. We're *both* accused of helping Tuthmosis escape. Tomb robbers are put to death. And death will be Tuthmosis's penalty if Wosret convinces Amenhotep and Nefertiti that he committed the robbery. There's no other option.'

'There's nothing I have to say.'

'Ta-Miu, listen to me. Tuthmosis was once your special friend. Do you *want* him to die?'

'Amenhotep would never send his brother to his death.' I blocked my ears. 'I don't have to listen to you. Keep your distance. Share my cell if you must. The fleas and lice will soon get to you. But stay away from me!' I flung myself face down onto the filthy pallet and tucked my arms over my head so I didn't have to hear her.

For a while there was silence. I could hear by the snoring coming from next door that the old woman was sound asleep. I raised my head slightly to get some air. Isikara was crouched on the stone floor staring ahead of her. But then I looked again. She was reading the words I'd carved into the walls.

I jumped up and spread my arms across them. 'By all that's holy – don't you *dare*! These are private thoughts. Not meant for you!'

Her eyes turned briefly to me and then went back to the words.

'I said . . . *Stop!*'

But she ignored me.

I stumbled across the floor to find the ankh and began jabbing at the words so I could obliterate them. 'You have no right. They're not meant for your eyes.'

'Who are they for, then?' She tossed her head and looked back at me. 'When you write words you have to be prepared for people to read them. Why *did* you write them?'

I spun around to face her. 'What do *you* know? You've never been in prison. I thought I'd die here and then what did it matter who read them? They're random words. They're just a jumble. They don't tell the whole story.'

'Then why did you write them?'

'I was trying to discover the truth in my head.'

'Have you?'

I clenched the ankh in my fist. Stared straight back at her.

She didn't turn away. 'Will the boy who stole the ring, the one you wrote of, the boy you told the secret to . . . will he come for you?'

'A pestilence of flies on you! You read everything!'

'Everything . . . except his name. Who is he?'

'Do you think I'd tell you?'

'You have to, if we're to escape.'

'Damn you!' I flung the ankh at her. It missed her head, hit the wall behind and fell to the floor. '*You . . .!*'

She picked the ankh up calmly and stared back at me, her eyes like dark emeralds flecked with particles of gold dust in the half-light. 'Yes . . .?'

'You left Thebes and now you think you can come back and see inside my head and tell me what I should do. I wish I'd never helped you escape with Tuthmosis. You come here fresh from Nubia and you judge me. But you know nothing about what's been happening in Thebes. *Nothing* at all!' I spat out the words.

'I know how evil Wosret can be.'

'How would you know? You've not been here!'

'Wosret's power extends far beyond Thebes. This proves it!' She thrust out her right hand. 'They took off my bow fingers in Nubia.'

I stared at the two fingers that ended abruptly at the

168

second knuckle. The scars were still red and raw and horrible to look at.

'The Nubians?'

'No, the Egyptians.'

Isikara didn't take her eyes from my face. 'So you told that boy a secret?'

'What if I did?' I felt my arms heavy at my sides.

'You told him about the key Tuthmosis gave you. The key to the labyrinth. Didn't you?'

'You're guessing. My words don't say that.'

'But they say you told him a *secret* you shouldn't have told. He's the tomb robber, isn't he?'

Her certainty angered me. Samut had held me in his arms. A fire had burned inside me. I trusted him with all my secrets. Why hadn't he trusted me with his?

I gave her a hard look and the words came out like bitter gall from the back of my throat. 'You don't know that for certain. Besides, I didn't give him the key.' I snatched the ankh from her hand and held it up. 'This key I'm holding . . . *this* is the one Tuthmosis gave me! See, I still have it!'

'I know you didn't give the boy *that* key.'

'Then how can you accuse me?'

'You didn't give the boy your *own* key. But you told him where to find the *other* key. The duplicate one that lay on the ledge inside the gate.'

'What? How do you know about that key?'

'You've forgotten. I've been in the labyrinth. I escaped with Tuthmosis using that exact key. Your friend – the one whose name you're so careful not to mention – used the duplicate key to enter the secret gate to King Amenhotep's tomb. *He's* the tomb robber. All you have to do now is speak out against him.'

Thoughts swirl in my head. I want to shut her up. I want to spring forward and tear out her throat. But the lioness spirit of Sekhmet fails me. Instead I thrust my ankh into the surface of the wall. 'Stand back!' I hiss. 'You're asking me to betray someone I love.'

'No, I'm asking you to protect someone who was once your friend. Tuthmosis is worth defending.'

CHAPTER NINETEEN

LADY OF FLAME

Kiya paced back and forth twisting the edge of her sleeve between her fingers. She couldn't gather her thoughts. They darted about like fireflies in her head. Tiny, bright thoughts that zigzagged back and forth, but seemed to go nowhere. How could she rescue Ta-Miu?

A maid sighed and nodded in her direction. 'What's to be done with her? Just look at what she's doing to that cloth. She'll tear it to shreds and then *we'll* have to mend it.'

'Do you think if we find her a second chameleon, she'll be distracted?' The other maid shrugged.

'Nothing will distract her while she's fretting over Ta-Miu.'

'Hah! Well, she'll wear out her sandals on that one too. Ta-Miu's not worth fretting about. She got what she deserves. She stole a ring!'

'You don't know that for sure. I smell a dead fish. I don't think the tomb robbery has anything to do with Ta-Miu. She's not the sort who would do something as shocking as steal from a tomb. I think she's innocent.'

'*Innocent?* A girl who runs off every afternoon to kiss a boy she hardly knows and leaves us to do all her work . . . *innocent?* Hah! And if she's so innocent, why's she in prison?'

'It was *you*, wasn't it? *You* told about the ring being under her bedclothes!'

'What if I did? She's the guilty one. She's the one who's in prison.'

'Just because someone's in prison doesn't make them *guilty!*' The maid reached out her hand to Kiya. 'My Lady, please stop! All that tearing at your sleeve won't return Ta-Miu to us.'

Kiya looked back at her blankly and then went on pacing.

Who could she appeal to? It was no use speaking to Nefertiti. It suited her to have Ta-Miu accused of stealing the ring. With the rumour of Tuthmosis's return, Nefertiti would be terrified he'd come to claim his throne. She'd be even more anxious to blame Tuthmosis for the tomb robbery. To have Ta-Miu accused of treachery made her argument against Tuthmosis all the stronger. And it would be hopeless trying to appeal to Wosret. He was aligned with Nefertiti.

Who then? There was only Amenhotep.

She snapped her fingers and swung around. *Yes*, that was it. 'Prepare a fresh robe. I must speak to the King.'

'What will you say, my Lady?'

Kiya flopped down onto her bed. 'Yes, what *will* I say? Oh Hathor, Protector of Women, help me. What must I say to Amenhotep? If only Ta-Miu were here to help me!'

'It's not Hathor you need now, my Lady. It's her fighting opposite spirit, Sekhmet the lioness, you must call on. The goddess Sekhmet will rise up and claw your enemies by the throat. Sekhmet's action is always right. She destroys with appropriate vengeance. Believe me, it's never chaotic or random. It's always what's needed at the time. I urge you. Call on her, rather than Hathor, to strike at your enemies.'

Kiya sighed from her curled-up position on the bed. 'Yes, I suppose, as I live and breathe, you're right.'

'Sekhmet removes every threat. She punishes all who do wrong against Maat. Implore her, the Lady of Flame, to be on your side when you speak to Amenhotep. Come, get up now! Wear your gilded silver pectoral inlaid with lapis lazuli and agate and your lioness amulet of gold to protect you.'

'Yes.' Kiya jumped up from the bed. 'I'll wear the pectoral and the lioness amulet and I'll call on Sekhmet to stand alongside me in her flame-red dress stained with the blood of her foes. I'll ask her to breathe on my enemies with the hot desert wind of her breath! Now prepare my robe. I'll wear the one threaded with red as well. Nefertiti will *not* dictate what I can or cannot wear tonight. With Sekhmet at my side I'll show my fighting spirit. I'll be strong.'

Then the maid leant forward and whispered in her ear. 'Remember too that the King is young and still a boy. Don't be too fiery. Beguile him with your own young and charming ways, Princess Tadukhepa.'

Despite the bravery in her rooms while she was bathing and preparing to see Amenhotep, now, as she stood waiting for him in the antechamber to his private quarters, Kiya felt nervous. How would the King receive her? And what would she say? And what if Nefertiti, the very person she most dreaded, accompanied him? Now she regretted the flamboyance of her red woven dress.

She glanced around at the grandeur of the chambers and wished she hadn't come alone. Some attendants would have given her courage. But the person she truly needed at her side now was Ta-Miu. Yet she was the *very* reason she was here.

Everything in the King's quarters was grand and lavish. The walls, painted the deepest blue, dark as the night, seemed to be made entirely of lapis lazuli and were embellished with gold stars. And hovering across the ceiling was the Vulture Goddess, Nehkbet, with huge outstretched wings inlaid with gold and turquoise and carnelian. And in each of the four corners of the room, a flaring golden cobra with ruby eyes rose up ready to strike at the King's enemies. On each snake's head was a gold sun-disc from behind which tongues of fire gave out a flickering light as if to enhance the cobra's power.

Kiya closed her eyes – all this splendour was making her dizzy. As she did so, she became aware of flute music floating into the room. But there'd been no sign of any flute players. Perhaps they were hidden behind the gold latticed screen that stood to one side. A fragrance of cinnamon and sandalwood wafted towards her.

Someone touched her shoulder. And when she opened her eyes again, Amenhotep was standing in front of her. By contrast to the magnificence of the room, he wore a white linen wrap tied simply around his hips with a single gold clip and his head was unadorned by either crown or even wig. He was unattended but had clearly come straight from his bath as his short hair was tousled and still wet and dripped down onto his shoulders. She could just catch the warm smell of sandalwood and cinnamon coming from his skin.

She dropped her eyes in confusion.

Amenhotep laughed. 'You seemed at peace. What were you dreaming?'

Kiya looked back up at him. He blinked and glanced quickly away. She hadn't realised how shy he was. Dressed in his usual fine robes and leopard cloak and the Double Atef Crown or the blue Warrior Crown of Egypt, he seemed much more robust and kingly than this young, handsome boy that stood in front of her with his dripping hair looking as if he'd just come from swimming with some friends in the river.

She suddenly remembered she should bow. 'No, my Lord, I was in fact dizzy.'

'Dizzy? Are you ill?'

She shook her head. 'No . . . confused, rather.'

'Confused?'

'I don't know what to do,' she suddenly blurted out and then was vexed with herself for sounding like a child.

'About what?'

By all that was holy, she truly wished Ta-Miu was with her. She felt so stupid for gabbling away like this. Yet the very person she needed was the person she was pleading for. 'I implore you to bring Ta-Miu back to the Palace. I can't cope without her.'

'But you have so many maids.'

She gave him a quick look. Was he laughing at her? She shook her head. 'It's not her services I need. It's her good advice.'

'Good advice?' He raised an eyebrow. 'From a tomb robber?'

Surely he was teasing her. She shook her head vigorously. 'You can't believe she robbed your father's tomb?' She wrinkled her nose in frustration. A pestilence! Now she'd spoken too forthrightly again!

'Who did, then?'

She bit her lip. It had been on the tip of her tongue to blurt out Samut's name. 'I can't say. But I beg you to be kind until all this is resolved. The prison is a terrible place.'

'How would you know?'

Would he laugh if she told him? 'I visited Ta-Miu disguised as her brother.' She rushed on before she could make any further mistakes. 'Please allow her to return to the Palace.'

He pulled a face as if sharing a secret. 'Nefertiti won't be happy.'

'If Ta-Miu can't return as my maid, allow her at least to work somewhere else in the Palace. But free her from the prison. She'll die there. Let her work in the weavery, or in the Unguent Rooms or the wig workshops. There must be *some* position that needs to be filled.'

He laughed as if he knew he shouldn't be laughing. 'Nefertiti wouldn't take kindly to Ta-Miu being her wigmaker. It has to be something that takes her out of sight.'

'So you *will* free her, then?' Without thinking Kiya took hold of Amenhotep's hands. Then suddenly realised what she'd done and felt the colour rise in her cheeks again. 'Forgive me.' She tried to pull away but Amenhotep held her firmly. He was an odd mixture. Shy but at the same time confident. It was hard to explain but there was some inner strength about him. A strength that came from the quiet way he held himself. He didn't blurt out words like she did.

'What work shall I give her? Should I send her to the potteries? She could learn to make floor tiles and decorate them. Would that suit you?'

Kiya bit her lip. 'The potteries are no place for a girl. The work is hard, the clay rough, and the heat of the kilns unbearable. Isn't there something gentler she can do?'

'What about the Unguent Rooms? She'd be surrounded by lilies and roses and exotic scents and flagons of precious oils.' Suddenly he seemed unsure of himself again and let go of her hands. 'Girls like that, don't they?'

'Perhaps Isikara can be sent as well. I've heard she has also been imprisoned.'

He shrugged. 'If that's what you wish. There can't be any harm. The Unguent Rooms are as safe as any prison.'

Kiya remembered to bow. 'You're very kind.'

'I used to watch you and Ta-Miu when Tuthmosis was showing off with his throwing stick and his archery skills.'

Kiya laughed. 'We were new to the Palace and easily impressed.'

'I was jealous of Tuthmosis. Our father chose to have him ride alongside on his chariot when he hunted. When Tuthmosis had his accident and his leg was broken and wouldn't heal and he had a fever, I hoped he'd die.' Amenhotep hesitated.

Kiya nodded to try and ease his shyness.

'I was even more jealous when I discovered you'd be Tuthmosis's wife after my father died. I wanted him dead once more. And then it happened, or so I was led to believe by Wosret. Finally he *was* dead! And I was drenched with terrible guilt that I'd brought on his death by my wishes. I vowed I'd rule as he would've ruled if he'd been King. Fairly and without war.'

She smiled. 'Well, now you are relieved of your guilt. Tuthmosis is alive after all.'

Amenhotep suddenly frowned. 'Yes, so I've heard. But all Nefertiti has in her head is that he's come to claim his throne. Do you think it's true? The throne *is* rightfully his. He might claim you back as well.'

'I'm your obedient servant. My father sent me from Mitanni to Egypt as a gift to the King. The King died and *you* are now my husband.'

'Yes but if Tuthmosis ruled Egypt, would you remain my wife?'

She tried to hide her smile at the seriousness of his question. Her maid had been only half right. She'd called on the lioness Sekhmet, Lady of Flame, to fight at her side. But now it seemed it was Sekhmet's opposite spirit, Hathor, Goddess of Love, who'd appeared as well this evening.

'I think I would.'

PART THREE

CHAPTER TWENTY

NEFERTITI'S CHAMBERS

Nefertiti sat stroking her cheetahs as they lolled across the pillows of her bed. 'What do you think, Wosret, is the King in love with that little princess from Naharin or in love with me?'

'I don't know why you bother about her. The King is in love with you. You will soon have his child to prove it.' He bowed his head and said quickly, 'May Hathor ensure it's a boy!'

Nefertiti's mouth twitched. 'The King was seen reading a note delivered by a secret messenger and I've heard that Princess Tadukhepa has visited his chambers.'

Wosret seemed startled. 'A note? I've heard of no note.'

'Well, there was one. It was given to my husband by a servant, who in turn told my servant. The note was sealed and no one had the courage to break the seal and read it before it was delivered. Do you think it was from Princess Tadukhepa?'

'Why would she send the King a note?'

'She's bold. She thinks she can get Amenhotep's attention. She's a scheming little desert fox. I can see it in those slanting eyes that try to appear so innocent.'

'Don't trouble yourself with her. She's very young.'

'But she vexes me!' Nefertiti sat up so abruptly that one of the cheetahs snarled. She turned and fondled its ears absent-mindedly and smoothed out the jewelled chain that hung around its neck. 'Wosret, find that note so we can see what she's written and why she visited him.'

'I'm sure you're mistaken. The note is probably only to ask for his clemency on behalf of her maid.'

'Surely not all that fuss again! The maid is a thief. She deserves to be locked up forever for being in possession of King Amenhotep's emerald ring.'

'Amenhotep thinks you are too rash.'

'Too rash?' Nefertiti sat up so abruptly that the cheetahs leapt from the bed and began stalking around the room. 'Too rash, when I've discovered she's secretly visited Amenhotep? And now the rumour of

Tuthmosis's return and him ready to snatch the crown!'

Her agitation was making the cheetahs snarl and hiss. Wosret stepped aside as they paced past him, their heavy tails swishing behind them. 'Can't you make these infernal animals lie down? They belong in a cage, not stalking around a bedchamber. And certainly not on your bed. Get them to lie down on their pillows.'

'They're only doing what cheetahs know to do. They're hunters. So they pace.'

'Well, train them to stand still. They make me nervous!'

'I thought nothing ever made you nervous!' Nefertiti gave a little laugh like the sound of her bangles jangling against each other.

Wosret shook his head impatiently as if he wanted the meeting to proceed. 'The matter of Tuthmosis is truly *serious*, Nefertiti. It's what I've come to see you about. I've tracked down the girl he ran away with, and have had her imprisoned.'

'The embalmer's daughter?'

Wosret nodded. 'Yes, Isikara. But she's a feisty girl and won't answer questions. And Tuthmosis gave my men the slip. He's gone into hiding and can't be found. There's a rumour he wants to meet his brother. We

EYE OF THE SUN

can't let him take the throne. If he does, your position is at stake.'

Nefertiti glanced up quickly. 'Surely there's a way around this?'

'How?'

'Could I become Tuthmosis's wife?'

'And leave Amenhotep?'

'You're clever, Wosret. You'll think of something.' She took hold of his hand. 'You're the Highest of High Priests, after all. You can arrange anything. Make sure I keep the crown!'

Wosret gave a little laugh, more a growl than true laughter. 'Nefertiti, you give me powers beyond my capability.'

'Yes, but the matter of Tuthmosis must be dealt with and dealt with quickly. One way or another, I *must* remain Queen. But first I want you to find the note from that Naharin girl. I want to discover what she has written to Amenhotep. There's too much at stake.'

CHAPTER TWENTY-ONE

THE UNGUENT ROOMS

The sound of rough voices woke me.

'Seems you are both important. Here's someone with a bunch of keys to unlock your cell! Oi! Where are you taking them?'

'None of your business, old woman!'

'What?' I shook Isikara. 'Wake up! We're being released!'

Two guards pulled us past the old woman's cell and for the first time I saw her face, lined and tired and ancient-looking from her seven years of hardship. Her hand reached out from between the bars as she tried to snatch at the guards. 'What's so important about the likes of *them*? What about *me*?'

Suddenly I felt guilty. 'I'll speak out for you, old

woman, I promise!' I called back over my shoulder.

I avoided all looks from Isikara. We were forced up some steps and marched outside without any answers to our questions. My eyes and ears hurt from the brightness and confusion and tumult in the street. I stumbled and was yanked up by the arm and trundled along the alleyways between people who stared and pointed. The sharp clank of the guards' weapons knocking against each other kept me in check. Where were they taking us?

Across the Great River the Theban hills quivered in the heat and the sun burnt hot on my shoulders as we were pushed on board a ferry. Still I avoided Isikara's eyes as we sat on opposite sides of the boat. On the western bank, we were put on donkeys and taken to the Palace. But once through the gates, we were led away from the road that led to Kiya's quarters and passed through another set of gates into a workshop area. Finally the donkeys were halted in a courtyard completely enclosed by mud-brick buildings and walls. A strong perfume of roses and lilies filled the hot, dry air, yet there was no sign of a garden.

Isikara nudged me and whispered, 'Where are we? Is this another prison?'

But I refused to answer even though I knew we were at the Palace Unguent Rooms.

She glanced about quickly and kept her voice low. 'We must grab the first chance we have to escape, so you can defend Tuthmosis.'

I gave her a sharp look. 'Don't be so sure! You forget. I haven't promised *anything* yet,' I hissed.

The guards spoke to a frail, elderly man. There were deep frown marks on his forehead as he looked in our direction. Then we were left in the courtyard, while they rode off on the donkeys and the gates were closed and locked behind them.

The old man stepped up close to peer at us. Or so I thought, until I realised he was blind as he stretched out his hand to touch our faces.

'I'm looking for a sign of your youth and the size of your noses. Only a good strong nose can create fragrances. Apart from a sensitive nose, you need a good memory and a prodigious ability to precisely describe scents.' He took a step back. 'Do the two of you have these qualities?'

It was unnerving having him stare at me when I knew he couldn't see me. I kept silent. Neither did Isikara answer.

'Hmmph! I thought so!' The old man shook his head wearily. 'There was a time when the job of a perfume maker was handed down from father to son but times have changed. And now they've sent me two girls! Two completely *inexperienced* prison girls and what must I do with you? What good are you? Noses must be trained to pick up scent like flypaper picks up flies. You've probably already allowed your sense of smell to be distracted by all sorts of odours and will hardly know a dead fish from a dead rat!'

I saw Isikara toss her head. 'I think I would! I trained as an embalmer.'

'Don't answer back. I won't take any nonsense. Especially from girls who have no sense of smell.'

'Who's to say we have no sense of smell?'

'I say so! You both stink. You are an unwashed riot of odours.'

'It was the prison! We had no access to water,' Isikara replied.

'Get to that stone trough over there, then,' he said brusquely. 'Scrub yourselves down with the swabu paste of ash and clay and put on the clean tunics you'll find hanging there, before you set foot in my Unguent Rooms.'

I sensed Isikara's eyes on me as I walked ahead.

'If we're to escape, we might as well try to be friends, Ta-Miu,' she whispered as soon as we were out of earshot.

I dunked my head into a trough of cold water and rubbed the swabu paste into the places on my scalp

192

that itched, annoyed that she should feel I could so easily be won over.

'Why do you suppose they've brought us here?'

I swept the wet hair back from my forehead. 'It was probably Kiya's work. But don't think we are *truly* released.'

Isikara glanced up from scrubbing at the dirt under her nails. 'Why do you say that?'

'Didn't you see the courtyard has locked gates?'

'So?'

'This courtyard is kept locked because of the secrets the workshops contain. Recipes for perfume made especially for the Palace. And in some case perfumes for only one individual. Queen Tiy had her own secret lily perfume made by the old man himself, and no other. His name is Intef.'

'What's that to do with us?' Isikara asked, as she pulled a clean tunic over her head and rearranged the folds.

'Everyone who works here is kept under lock and key, to prevent them giving out the secrets.'

The old man, Intef, suddenly appeared in the doorway. His sight might have been impaired but his hearing was good. 'Your friend is right. Perfume makers are always confined. They ply their trade under lock and key in this guarded courtyard to safeguard the secrets of the Palace perfumes. Revealing Unguent Room secrets is punishable by death.'

I glanced across at Isikara to see how she was taking this news. Kiya might have freed us from real prison but this was just another sort.

Isikara shrugged and whispered, 'At least it's a *perfumed* prison! We have to be clever and use every opportunity to our best advantage. Make yourself pleasant.'

I gave her a look. Who was *she* to tell *me* to look pleasant?

As we entered the first room the odours were overwhelming. Sharp shafts of sunlight sliced through the room. As my eyes became accustomed to this, I saw it was some sort of storeroom. Shelves were stacked with bundles of bark. Bunches of grasses and herbs hung from the ceiling. Wicker trays were piled high with dried rose petals. And everywhere there were containers of dark, twisted roots, jars of black berries, flagons of oil and stone basins that held lumps of amber-coloured resin as large as my fist that glimmered like jewels when they caught a streak of sunlight.

Above or next to each type of plant or petal or pod were paintings on the walls that showed each growing in their natural state with their leaves and berries and roots all in place. And attached to every bundle or basket or flagon, were labels with hieroglyphic inscriptions like 'Scented Giu grass from the oases', 'Roots of the Bearded Iris', 'Aromatic Nubian rush', 'Sef wan oil from the wood of the Syrian juniper', 'Root of Indian Spikenard', 'Crocus stamens for khypri' and 'Oil of Mereh nar kernels'. It was like reading a language that belonged in a strange, foreign country.

'Come over here!' Intef commanded. 'Close your eyes and hold a piece of this bark, one in each hand, and tell me the difference.'

The two-finger length quills of bark he handed us looked almost identical. One was slightly darker but otherwise there was no telling the difference.

'They're both cinnamon bark,' I said.

'No!' Intef shook his head. 'Don't make snap decisions.'

I glanced at Isikara. Her eyes were still closed and she was breathing evenly and deeply, sniffing each quill in turn. 'My left hand holds cinnamon but the one in my right hand is different. Hotter. More pungent. Almost rose smelling. It's not cinnamon. It's cassia bark.'

'*What?*' The old man turned his head sharply as if he would've stared in amazement if he could have, except his eyes were milky as usual. 'How did you know that? Have you worked with unguents before?'

Isikara nodded. ' I told you before. My father was the embalmer, Henuka.'

'Henuka? The High Priest at the Temple of Sobek? I knew him well. We exchanged methods and recipes.'

Isikara looked puzzled. 'I've never met you before.'

'Don't be silly, girl!' He sounded vexed. 'Of course you wouldn't have met me. I've lived here at the Unguent Rooms all my life. As Holder of the Recipes of Secret Perfumes I've never been allowed further than this courtyard.'

'Never ever been further than this courtyard?'

Intef shook his head. 'I corresponded with your father secretly through a scribe. We followed the same beliefs. If you've learnt at your father's side, you'll be a good alchemist. But your friend from Naharin will have to work in the flower-pressing room. Her nose has no flare for odours.'

Isikara was showing off and now I was being dismissed! 'How do you know I won't learn? And how do you know I'm from Naharin?'

'The answer to both questions is, I hear by your voice. When you're blind, your ears tell you what your eyes cannot see.'

'But that was just *bark*. I know grasses and flowers.

196

I've sat in fields of flowers that are as vibrant as to burn the eyes . . .' I bit my lip realising the stupidity of speaking about colours.

Isikara interrupted. 'I returned to Thebes to take over my father's position at the Temple of Sobek. I can't remain here.'

Intef shrugged. 'That may be so, but the god Sobek has fallen out of favour. Besides, the Highest of High Priests has other plans for you!'

'Wosret? What are his plans?'

The old man waved his arms with agitation as if trying to waft odours and perfumes around to present them to a client. 'It's not for me to say.'

CHAPTER TWENTY-TWO

THE PALACE STABLES

Nefertiti rose while the early morning mist still hung low over the river. She dressed in a plain unadorned tunic and had one of her serving women arrange a simple wig on her head. The garden in her courtyard was bathed in cool green light but already she could see the quivering heat haze beginning to rise from the stone paving. The day was going to be scorching hot.

With a wave of her hand she bade the serving women to stand aside and set out alone to accomplish her plan.

It was time to make the ride to the Temple of Amun – not standing alongside Amenhotep in his chariot but driving her *own* horses in her *own* chariot. The chariot was newly-built and painted and gilded and stood ready, waiting for the right moment. Now, with the heavens pouring forth their golden light and the waters of the Great River shimmering back, it was time. She would ride out and greet the sun.

She would show Thebes she was worthy of admiration and adoration. The unveiling of the new Royal Temple of Gempaaten would be celebrated with a chariot driven by their Queen. From the moment she stepped off the Royal Barge, she would lead the procession up through the sphinx-lined avenue, the only woman driving a chariot, to the great gate posts of the Temple of Amun, for all to see she was Queen of the land. Queen of the gods.

It was a good plan, well thought out and entirely devised by herself . . . not thought up by Wosret for a change.

She walked slowly around the lake. Beyond the formal gardens, she came to the stables with its raw smell of oats and straw and horses. The courtyard was empty as she entered and stood looking about her. She had chosen her own pair of horses for her chariot. A pair of matching chestnut stallions, that the old Naharin horse handler had said were not too frisky but yet fiery and powerful enough to look magnificent in a parade.

Suddenly Nefertiti became aware of movement at the far end of the stalls. A stable boy was brushing down a horse. She approached quietly and watched as his hands worked expertly over the flank of a milk-white horse.

'You do that well. That's one of the new Assyrian horses.'

He dropped the brush and stood up quickly as she spoke.

'There's no need to stop.' He was older than she had at first thought and had a certain arrogance as he looked at her with his shoulders thrown back.

'You're too early if you are looking for any of the horse handlers or the stable vizier. There's no one here.'

'Except you.'

He twitched his shoulders impatiently.

'Then don't let me stop you from your work. I've come to see my horses.'

'*Your* horses?' he snorted. 'These horses here all belong to the new King.'

She narrowed her eyes and then laughed. 'And the new Queen! Don't forget she owns them as well.'

'Yes, she has two stallions. But of course they're just for show. She's fond of putting up a show. I've never seen her with them. I don't think she knows a thing about horses. She isn't the type. She doesn't care much for horses if you ask me.'

'I didn't ask you but since you've told me, *I've* seen her with them. They're chestnut stallions.'

'Have you now?' He stood a step closer and put his hand on her arm. 'Well then, you keep a closer watch on the Queen than I. I've never seen her here at the stables. If you know so much you must be one of her maids. But if you're a maid, and a very attractive maid at that, why would you be here talking about horses and flirting with me? Why wouldn't you be in her quarters attending to her demands?'

'A *maid*? And *flirting*? With *you*!' She flashed her eyes at him. And then checked herself. Yes. Why not? Why *shouldn't* she play a little teasing game? He was handsome after all. She smiled. 'Judging by the height of the sun, the Queen's probably still fast asleep in her quarters.'

'They say she's very demanding and spoilt and—' He stopped brushing abruptly and glanced at her. 'You're not going to repeat all this to her, are you?'

She tried to hide her smile and shook her head. 'There'd be no need.'

'No need?' A sudden look of surprise crossed his face as if someone had thumped him from behind. He stood upright and stared back at her. And then took a quick step backwards. 'You're not?'

She stood laughing at him and nodded.

'Don't fool with me! You're like any girl. Just setting out to tease!' He reached out and took hold of her shoulders and turned her around to face the sunlight. 'I'd know if—' Then his hands sprang away from her shoulders as if burnt by the touch of her skin. They fell helplessly to his sides. 'By my breath, I'm done for! That perfume! I should have recognised that perfume. You wore it on the Royal Barge that day on the river. It floated back to me afterwards. Lilies and bergamot and fragrances the nose can't even begin to describe. And now here you are! *Queen Nefertiti!* In real life! And up close, you're even more beautiful than . . .'

'Than?' Her eyes questioned his. Was he confused? Or was he flirting with her?

He looked about hurriedly as if sure someone would come and smite him down. Then he fell to the straw at her feet. 'Forgive me! I'm done for!'

She tipped the toe of her sandal at his shoulder. 'Get up, stupid boy! You don't have to do that. I could have you whipped. But I knew you hadn't guessed my secret. And I was playing a game. I wanted to see how long it would take you.'

'But why? And where are your attendants? I'll be in serious trouble for talking to you.' He stood up and turned away abruptly.

'Wait!' She took hold of his chin and turned his face back to hers. 'Don't dare turn away from me! You'll be in serious trouble for *not* talking to me! Where are my horses?'

'Over there in the stables.'

'Over there in the stables, my *Queen*, is what you're supposed to say! Take me to them, then.'

'It's better if you wait for the stable vizier.'

She raised her eyebrows. '*My Queen!*'

He bowed. 'It's better if you wait for the stable vizier, my Queen.'

She flicked at a piece of straw that had stuck to his leather boot, with the tip of her sandal. 'I'm Queen. I wait for no one. I want to see them *now*. What's your name?'

He shook his head. 'There's no need of a name.'

'My *Queen*!' she insisted then shrugged. 'Well, I'm ordering you . . .' She couldn't stop a smile creeping across her face. 'No, perhaps I'm *asking* you to take me to my horses.'

His eyes travelled slowly over her. Nefertiti stood her ground and watched him surveying her. This boy was handsome. She was pleased she'd worn a very light and cool linen robe with no other adornment. Its pleats hung well and showed the curves of her body to their best advantage.

When his eyes reached hers she thought he would blush but he showed no signs of being ill at ease for having been caught out in his scrutiny. Instead there was a faint smile curling the corners of his lips. She lifted an eyebrow and returned his glance.

'What about your thin sandals and the edges of your robe? You're not attired for entering a stable.'

She tossed her head. 'No matter. I want to discuss how the horses must be dressed when they draw my chariot to the Temple of Amun for the unveiling of the new Gempaaten Temple tomorrow.'

'Who will be your driver?'

'I will be my *own* driver.'

She bent down to stroke a cat that was rubbing itself against her legs.

'You'll drive your own chariot?'

She looked up from the cat and saw the amazement in his eyes and nodded.

He smiled broadly for the first time. 'You've a keen eye for a horse. You've chosen your pair of stallions well.'

'I thought the Queen knew *nothing* about horses!' she teased.

He bowed. 'I'm suitably rebuked.' Then he stood back to allow her to enter the stable first and pointed to two stalls alongside each other. 'They're tethered but be careful. They're powerful horses and could harm you if they reared.'

Nefertiti laughed as she touched the arched, swan neck of the closest horse. 'I like their rich colour. I think leopard-skin head-gear with plumes of ostrich and a red tasselled cloak is what is needed for each horse. What do you think will show to the best advantage?'

He lounged up against the door frame and laughed suddenly as her eyes challenged his. 'Whose best advantage? *Yours* or the horses?'

She gave him a sidelong look. Now who was teasing whom? For a stable hand he certainly had swagger. Enough swagger to be her chariot runner. He'd make a handsome boy at her side. She could flaunt him every day in front of the ladies on the way to the Temple. They would love him.

'I want you as my chariot runner. I'll give you one of my pet cheetahs to run alongside you.' Her eyes flashed in the dim light of the stables as she looked directly at him. 'I dare you to accept!'

They both turned as the noise of someone entering the courtyard interrupted them.

'We have company. A pity, our interlude is over.' Then she looked directly at him again. 'I could order your obedience you know!'

He gave a curt bow, then turned and hastily disappeared out of a side door that led away from the courtyard. At the same moment the main entrance to the stables was blocked by the frame of a large man.

'Your Majesty!' The stable vizier drew a sharp, deep breath and tugged clumsily at his tunic to check it was properly tied before he bowed and entered. 'This is unexpected. Had I known you'd planned to visit us so early, I'd have been here to receive you, my Queen.' He waved his arms about as if swatting at gnats. 'What can I do for you? What can I show you? Where are your attendants? And won't your sandals be ruined?'

She shrugged. 'Sandals are easily replaced. I came to check whether my horses and chariot will be ready.'

'But you could've sent a messenger. And ready? Ready for *what*, my Queen?'

'I'll be driving my chariot tomorrow to the unveiling of the new Royal Temple of Gempaaten.'

'But I wasn't informed.'

'You're being informed now! See it is ready.'

He bowed. 'Everything has been done to your exact

instruction. The chariot has been gilded and painted with your cartouche and the wheels are of the latest design, six-spoked, each spoke light and well-shaped, with a woven carriage for delicacy and lightness, so the horses will appear as if they are carrying no more than a feather.' He bowed. 'Which indeed is the case, my Queen. But . . .'

'But what?'

'Should you be driving yourself? Is it safe?'

'Of course it is! I hope you've made sure the chariot doesn't squeak. I can't abide creaking chariots that screech at every wheel turn. It truly vexes me. Amenhotep's chariot was creaking yesterday like an old man's bones. It turns a chariot ride into a debacle. I expected people to start laughing at any moment.'

'I'm sorry you were vexed, my Queen. We've lined your chariot's hubs and axle with copper plates so there'll be no screech of wood against wood and the wheels have rawhide lashed to them to make them more silent.'

'Well, make sure the lashing doesn't wear away. I don't want the sound of flapping rawhide following me along the way!'

He bowed. 'The lashing is set in grooves to prevent wear. It won't break. And the harnesses for the horses have been made with especially dyed calfskin and have been studded with silver and the horses will be wearing ivory blinkers.'

'Good! I've instructed your stable boy that I want them dressed with ostrich plumes and tasselled cloaks as well.'

The vizier looked puzzled. 'My stable boy? No stable boy has arrived yet.'

She waved her hand. 'Well, I spoke to someone. He'll tell you what I want. He was here a moment ago.' Nefertiti gathered her robe to prevent it dragging in the straw and indicated she wished to pass. 'Make certain my chariot doesn't squeak!'

CHAPTER TWENTY-THREE

THE UNGUENT ROOMS

Isikara and I were put to work by Intef. I was sent to the flower-press room and Isikara to the main Unguent Room, where she worked at a bench blending oils and grinding resins and weighing powders on a balance, like Thoth making his judgements.

We hardly saw one another and at night we were so tired we fell asleep without speaking. Intef was strict with us. When the rose petals were delivered by the gardeners early each morning to the courtyard, we weren't allowed to waste time gossiping. I eyed the gardeners, trying to choose one who might bring me word of Samut, while the girls whispered instructions to me.

'Spread them on the tables under the reed awnings

before they bruise. They must be left just long enough for the sun to dry the dew but not long enough for the petals to go limp.'

'Do you ever get the chance to talk to the gardeners?' I whispered.

They shook their heads.

'Never?' My heart sank.

The girl next to me smiled and whispered, 'We don't have to *talk*! We use sign language. That way Intef doesn't know we're gossiping or goggling at one another!'

'I'm trying to find news of a boy called Samut.'

She laughed. 'Samut? You don't have to ask the *gardeners*. We know Samut well.'

I looked around at the group of them as their hands flew over the petals. '*We?* Do *all* of you know him?'

A girl shrugged. 'He's the biggest flirt in Thebes. There's probably not one girl in this courtyard who he hasn't kissed.'

I felt all the breath leave me as I stared around. 'He's kissed *all* of you?'

The girl next to me shrugged. 'What's a kiss from a boy as handsome as Samut?' Then she stopped briefly and searched my face. 'What do you want with him? You're not in *love* with him, are you? He's not worthy of true love.'

'Stop all this idle chatter and get off to the press room,' Intef growled. 'There are petals that have been steeping overnight, waiting to be squeezed out. And mind you rub out the collecting vessels with honey first and rub your hands properly with honey too before you toss today's petals in the oil. Be sure to follow the recipe exactly. Get along with you now. Stop all this chattering like a troop of monkeys.'

The girls moved quickly to the press room where the recipe for rose oil was painted on one of the mud walls.

2 baskets of camel grass bruised and
macerated and boiled up with:
9 jugs of green olive oil
1000 rose petals steeped in the above
Honey sufficient for coating hands and vessels
Salt as a fixative to prevent spoilage
Alkanet roots to make a red dye tincture

There were other recipes written up as well. One for lily oil and one called The Royal which had so many ingredients that the list went right down to the floor. It was almost as if every source of aroma that could be gathered from every part of the world was put into it. But it was rose oil we were making today.

I couldn't concentrate as the girls gathered large linen bags and lifted the steeping jars from the day before. They sieved the petals and oil that had turned golden through the linen bags into a huge jar smeared with honey. Then they twisted a stick into each corner of a bag and showed me how to get the last drop of essence from the mixture.

'Twist as hard you can as if you are wringing out washing.'

But I hardly heard what they said as I twisted with all the anger that welled up inside me. Samut could *never* have kissed them all!

'Here let me take over,' one of the girls offered. 'Your hands will get used to it eventually and calluses form where you once had blisters.'

While I stood watching the golden liquid drip into the vessel below, a girl at my side gave me a look. 'You're the Naharin girl, aren't you? The one they arrested for stealing a ring?'

'I didn't steal it.'

'No matter. We all know *who* stole it.'

'It wasn't stolen. It was a copy of the real ring.'

'A copy?' She gave me a look. 'He really *has* fooled you.'

'Who?'

'Samut, of course! I heard you talking about him.

212

He stole it, didn't he? We all know he's a tomb robber.'

I looked at her sharply. '*How* do you know?'

'Do you think he hasn't charmed us all with his trinkets?' She nodded her head towards a girl twisting a stick. 'Where do you think she got that charm around her neck?'

I stared back at her, my voice hardly daring to whisper, my stomach sick at the thought. 'From Samut?'

She nodded and whispered hurriedly, 'Make yourself busy. Here comes Intef.' Then she spoke louder for his benefit. 'This is the first oil but the same rose petals get steeped in fresh oil again and are squeezed once more for the second oil.'

Intef nodded. 'Four times with the same petals and then the oil is dyed with alkanet because its colour reflects the redness of the rose. Colour and clarity are as important as smell.'

'But . . .'

He waved his hand. 'Yes, I know what you're thinking. I can't see the clarity so how will I *know*. But no one wants a murky perfume the colour of mud. And least of all Nefertiti! I can *smell* murkiness! So watch out for sloppy work.'

I looked down at the blisters that were beginning to

form on my hands. All for the benefit of Nefertiti!
A pestilence of flies on her!

When Intef left, the girl nudged me. 'Your friend,
that girl working on the bench in the Unguent Room,
do you think she's noticed that all the other workers
alongside her are blind?'

'Are you sure?'

'Of course I'm sure! Only blind people are
employed on the bench. It's said they've a better sense
of smell because they aren't distracted. We call them
sniffers. None of the flower-press girls ever want to be
sniffers!'

'Why not?'

'There's too much at stake. If you're good, they
blind you to improve your sense of smell.'

'What? That can't be true! I don't believe you!'

She shrugged. 'You haven't worked here long
enough.'

'But surely they're employed in the Unguent
Rooms because they're *born* blind, like Intef?'

She nodded. 'Most, but not *all*!'

That night as we lay on our pallets in the workers'
quarters, I felt I had to warn Isikara. 'Pretend you're
hopeless.'

'In the name of Horus, why? I'm enjoying what I'm
doing. It's as good as making arrows when I was a

fletcher with the Nubian army. Why should I pretend I'm hopeless?'

I told her what the girl had said.

'Did you ask her to swear by Maat's feather?' she whispered.

I shook my head. 'I forgot.'

'Well, see then. It *can't* be true. She's wrong! Intef would *never* agree to have me blinded. He knew my father. And besides, Tuthmosis wouldn't allow it.'

'So where *is* Tuthmosis? He hasn't come to rescue you.'

'Well, nor has your friend, has he?' she hissed back at me. 'Tuthmosis is hiding until he's managed to speak to Amenhotep.'

'That's no help! If he's skulking and hiding, how'll he know they plan to blind you?'

'He's *not* skulking! And they're *not* going to blind me! Intef has found out I can read. He's selected certain scrolls for me to study. They were written up by the scribe who follows him around making notes. They're kept in sealed boxes in the Chamber of Secrets below the Unguent Rooms. *The Book of Heavenly Oils*, *The Book of Unguents for Unsealing the Heart* and *The Book of Moon Secrets*. Did you know unguents are made according to the moon cycles? It's all written in hieratic script and is easy to follow even though some words are strange and foreign. So why would he blind me? If I was blinded I wouldn't be able to read them.'

'That's *exactly* the point. He's given you the scrolls to read so you can commit the recipes and ingredients to memory, *before* you're blinded.'

'You're wrong. Intef wouldn't do that!'

'How can you be so sure?'

'I've discovered his secret. He needs me.'

'What's his secret?'

'He's anosmic.'

'Anosmic? What's that?'

'He's lost his sense of smell.'

'*What?* I don't believe you! When we arrived he said we stank!'

'Shhh! Keep your voice low. He was bluffing. He knew we wouldn't have washed in prison. And it's true. I've been watching the way he works. He simply carries on from memory, creating perfumes which he presents with great gravity pretending to sniff as he waves the odour around the room. But he no longer knows for sure. He can't smell *anything*.'

'But how can you be a perfume maker if you can't see and you can't smell?'

'*Precisely!* I'm the only one to have guessed his secret because the others can't see how puzzled his face sometimes looks. So he needs me to be his eyes *and* his nose. He won't have me blinded.'

'You can't rely on it!' Suddenly a thought struck me and my chest tightened as I lay in the darkness, letting the horror of it sink in. 'And it won't only be *you* they'd blind. You said yourself. Nefertiti has accused us *both* of helping Tuthmosis.'

Isikara pulled her sleeping pallet closer to mine. 'Don't fret, Ta-Miu,' she whispered. 'Nefertiti won't do it. What's got into you? Why're you so jumpy? We'll escape soon. I'll think of something. This isn't a prison.'

'Well, it seems like one! We're locked up and these girls are full of stories of being blinded and more . . .'

'More stories? About what?'

'About . . .' Without planning to I found I was telling her about Samut. In the darkness I couldn't see her expression. At first I didn't say his name. But then finally I did say Samut's name. And all the time I kept wishing I could stop. But I couldn't. And all the time I kept thinking she would say, *You deserved this! You told a secret you shouldn't have told.* But she didn't. And all the time I thought she would interrupt and say he was a rogue and not worth defending and that I should speak out against him. But she kept silent and listened while I talked and talked. Until eventually

217

I blurted out, 'And the flower-room girls say Samut has kissed them *all*.'

And then in the darkness, I heard Isikara finally begin to laugh. 'So *that's* what's got into you! You're jealous!'

CHAPTER TWENTY-FOUR

GEMPAATEN – HOUSE OF THE SUN-DISC

The hot sultry night brought little sleep to Nefertiti. Not even the slightest breeze wafted up from the river as she tossed about on her bed. Wosret had seen to it that the girl Isikara had been arrested for helping Tuthmosis escape. But now she'd heard that, unexpectedly, both Isikara and Tadukhepa's maid had been taken from prison and moved to the Palace perfumery.

The order could only have come from Amenhotep. But it had to be Tadukhepa who had persuaded him.

Nefertiti tossed this way and that, as thought followed thought as fast as falcons after prey and idea sparked idea and plan was added to plan. Her decision was the right one. Today she would begin its

EYE OF THE SUN

execution. Whatever might happen she was prepared.

As soon as the stars faded she called her chief attendant. 'Sitra, make preparations for today when we celebrate the new Gempaaten Temple. Be sure everyone is ready. The fan-bearers, the cheetah handlers, my grooms and chariot runners. Nothing must go wrong. They must all be in their places.'

'It's all arranged, my Lady, as we discussed yesterday.'

'And see that the gold menat necklaces for distribution are ready and the bouquets for the offerings are fresh. I want red poppies and bright blue cornflowers so they show up against my robe. Also see that the women who play the sistrums have checked them. I can't abide rusty rattles that have no tune to them.'

'I ordered new copper sistrums to be made. They've been coated with electrum so they'll catch the sunlight and reflect the glory of Aten. And each and every disc has been checked to see it runs freely on the wires.'

Nefertiti smiled. 'You've thought of everything, Sitra. I'll need two crowns. The Khepresh Warrior Crown with red streamers when I drive my chariot and the Double Atef Crown with the tall plumes and sun-disc for the ceremonies when our new Temple to the Sun is unveiled.'

'Both are prepared and are ready on their stands and I've chosen a bombyx silk for you to wear, fine and transparent as cobweb. Don't be nervous, my Lady. Everything will go smoothly.'

'I'm not nervous, Sitra. I just want perfection. Everyone must know I'm the Queen of Two Lands. Mistress of Egypt.'

'They will love you. The crowds are *already* gathering. I've heard they are lining the Palace road all the way to the banks of the river and gathering on the other side as well. There has never been a Queen so adored in Egypt.'

'Let it remain so. Is there any more news of Tuthmosis? What's the Palace gossip?'

'Don't worry. He can't take the throne from you now. You are too adored. The people of Thebes would *never* allow it.'

'But Sitra, why has he returned? Why didn't he stay in Nubia?'

'Don't fret now, my Lady.' She rested her hands firmly on Nefertiti's shoulders. 'You don't want creases on your forehead, today. Thebes is waiting for their beautiful Queen.'

When all was done and she stepped from her bath and was clothed and the Painter of the Eyes added the final sweep of galena paste to her eyelids and the

Painter of the Mouth made the final stroke of colour
on her lips, Nefertiti took one last look in her silver
hand-mirror set with its circlet of amethysts, then
smiled at Sitra and walked out from her courtyard.

She was ready to dazzle them all.

Amenhotep was standing waiting beside the double
palanquin reserved for special occasions, wearing
the elaborate Triple Atef Crown flanked by rising
cobras and topped with falcons bearing a sun-disc and
a double cartouche. A leopard cloak was slung over
his shoulder with the head and paws of the animal
hanging heavily across his chest and the eyes set with
two magnificent sparkling emeralds. The clasp holding
the skin and the gold belt circling his waist and the
wide armbands above his elbows and pectoral collar
on his broad chest, all glittered and flashed with gems.

Nefertiti caught his eyes and smiled as they bowed
formally to one another. He looked exceedingly
handsome and much older than his fifteen years. For a
moment she forgot her flirtation with the stable boy
and forgot too that she should be cross with him for
freeing Isikara and Ta-Miu from prison – life in the
Unguent Rooms was too easy.

They were helped into the great golden palanquin
with its protective lion figures and striking cobras
which took fifteen men to lift. Nefertiti wrapped her

arm around Amenhotep's waist to steady herself, while the bearers hoisted the poles up on their shoulders. Led by ten fan-bearers and priests swinging purifying censers, they were carried across a second courtyard towards the great double cedar doors of the Inner Palace where servants and attendants and bodyguards carrying bows and shields and wearing feathers in their hair to mark the celebration stood waiting to join the retinue.

Nefertiti heard the clamour of the waiting crowds outside the Palace and felt a shiver of anticipation run through her. Then the great outer gates were flung open wide and a roar of delight greeted her.

She smiled and took Amenhotep's hand as he helped her from the palanquin. 'We have to speak,' she said under her breath as she turned to wave at the cheering crowd.

Amenhotep nodded and smiled in all directions. 'What's so urgent that cannot wait until after the ceremony?'

'You've allowed the two girl prisoners to go free.'

'They're hardly free. They're working in the Unguent Rooms under lock and key. We can discuss this later.'

Beyond them the chariots for the entire procession stood lined up and gleaming in the sunshine behind pairs of horses that stamped and chafed at being held back by their handlers. Nefertiti's chariot was not in the lead as she had ordered but behind Amenhotep's. She strode towards it without waiting for him. A groom helped her mount the small step at the back. Then she took up the reins and edged the horses forward so that the chariot stood in line with his.

A smile crept across her face as she looked across at Amenhotep. 'Let's have some fun. Let's have a race! Just you and I.' Without waiting, amidst cheering and drumbeats and dust, she cracked her whip. Her chestnut horses sprang forward with her chariot runner up ahead leading a cheetah and her horse handler running alongside her. Officials and body-guards, taken by surprise, tried to keep back the throng of people in her pathway.

As the horses gathered speed, Nefertiti sensed the ribbons on her blue Warrior Crown and the silk of her robe streaming out behind her. She sensed too the appreciation of the crowd in the blur of faces and movement as they clapped and cheered and urged her on. With the hot wind against her face, she glanced sideways to see Amenhotep gaining on her.

'My Lady, my Lady! Slow down!' the horse handler shouted as he gasped for breath alongside the flying hooves and tried to keep up. But she cracked her whip and clung to the rail of her chariot, laughing as the horses galloped all the faster through the passageway between the people, her cheetahs striding far out in front of the runner who had fallen behind. Suddenly, she thought of the stable boy. She wished she'd *commanded* him to be her runner. He would've added a final flourish to the scene.

But for now she had made her point. Her plans were coming together. All of Thebes would love her. Now the next step was to deal with the two girls.

They drew up breathlessly at the quayside to board the Royal Barge which would take them across the Great River and up the canal, right to the quayside of the Temple of Amun.

As her feet touched the ground she glanced playfully back at Amenhotep. 'That was fun. Did you enjoy it?'

'Should a Queen do that? Do you think it was wise?'

'Wise? How can a race be wise?' She laughed and then shrugged. 'Who wants to be wise when you can have fun?' Her breath was still coming in gasps.

'You might have fallen and hurt yourself. And now especially . . .' But his voice trailed off in confusion.

Nefertiti sidled up to him and touched his cheek. 'Now we are to have a baby?' She straightened his crown that had been swept slightly to the side. 'You're *so* handsome today in your cloak and finery.' She looked up straight into those remarkable blue eyes so like his brother's and caught the flash of admiration in them before she turned and stepped on board the *Dazzling Aten.*

Her attendants quickly changed her Warrior Crown for the double-feathered Atef Crown and rearranged her robe, so that she was just in time to take up position under the red canopy of the Royal Barge at Amenhotep's side as they sailed alongside the Temple of Amun's quay to be greeted by even larger and more boisterous crowds.

The chariots and horses had been ferried across and were already waiting on the quayside to carry them along the unending avenue of sphinx-headed rams, with its paving already sprinkled with sacred oils, towards the great entrance of the Temple.

Now the pace of the chariots was slow and leisurely while women rattling sistrums went before them and priests purified the air ahead with swinging censers. Nefertiti smiled and waved in all directions as the crowds craned their necks to see through the clouds of swirling, fragrant incense smoke and reached out to try and touch the spoke of a wheel or the tassel of a tunic as they passed.

At the entrance to the Great Hypostyle Hall with its

high ceiling and gigantic columns, the chariots halted. Wosret came forward in his priestly leopard cloak and greeted them with a bow.

'I heard the crowd's appreciation. It seems you've tamed the people of Thebes,' he whispered to Nefertiti. Then he nodded at Amenhotep. 'Shall we proceed?'

He led them forward through the darkness of the Hall lit by flares that seemed to accentuate the great height of the columns and the ceiling so far above their heads. As they came to the gate built by Amenhotep's father, Nefertiti drew up sharply. Her eyes swept over the words that told of her father-in-law's greatness.

> *I, Amenhotep, King of Upper and Lower Egypt, ruler of Thebes, have built this monument to Amun and made a great Barque of new cedar, which was dragged over the mountains by the princes of all countries. There is none like it. Its hull is adorned with silver, wrought with gold throughout, and its shrine coated with electrum, so that it fills the land with its brightness.*

Nefertiti cast a moody eye across the carving of the barque below, which showed the old King holding the steering oar, while a human-headed sphinx with a cheetah's body perched on his roost in the prow of the barque above a wedjat eye.

'These inscriptions and carvings must be changed to include mine and my husband's names!'

Wosret sighed. 'All in good time! All in good time, Nefertiti! Today we celebrate your new Temple complex, Gempaaten, where there are plenty of inscriptions to you. But first we must placate Amun.'

They proceeded to the bolted entrance of the great cedar-wood door that led to the Innermost Sanctuary of the Amun. Wosret cleansed the air with burning incense, then he asked Amenhotep to break the clay seal on the lion-shaped bolt before they entered the Holiest of Holy Places, where no other person could enter except the King and Queen and he, Wosret, the Highest of High Priests.

It was built of sandstone from the Red Mountain and was lined with shining electrum and in it stood the statue of Amun alongside a lyre made of silver, gold, lapis lazuli and green malachite. Amenhotep held up his hawk-headed censing-spoon, filled with burning spices of myrrh and khypri, and made prayer offerings. Then Nefertiti stepped forward and laid down the huge bouquet of red poppies, cornflowers, lilies and lotus flowers on the offering table and made her incantation.

Then Wosret led them out into a courtyard on the eastern side along a walkway to the royal Temple of Gempaaten, built by the order of the new King, Amenhotep the Younger, to worship the Sun itself, Aten. It faced east to catch the first of Aten's rays and was so newly built that grains of sand still crunched on the paving under their sandals and its halls still smelt of newly-hewn stone and gardeners had barely had time to transform the mudflats around it into a place of greenery.

They took up their places on the Balcony of Appearances and rested their elbows on the squashy red bolsters that lined the parapet and looked down on the crowds that were pushing forward into the courtyard below. A deafening din of shouts of welcome, greetings and shrieks of delight, applause and cheering rose up and almost drowned the sounds of the flutes, tambourines, lutes, lyres and a harp so large it was played by two musicians on either side of it.

Nefertiti took the gold crescent-shaped menat necklaces encrusted with jewels that Sitra and the other attendants were holding, and held each one high so that it glittered and sparkled in the sunlight like a crescent sun. Then, with a smile just as dazzling, she tossed each one down separately in every direction

229

while people clamoured and grabbed and blessed her for her benevolence.

Out of the corner of her eye she suddenly caught sight of the other wives standing to the side watching. Amongst them was the pretty little princess from Naharin and she was reminded of what she still had to say to Amenhotep.

Alongside her, Amenhotep smiled and waved, mesmerised by the excitement of the people below.

'Listen to me, Amenhotep. They must be blinded!' Nefertiti said.

He turned distractedly. 'Blinded? Who? All these people? What do you mean?'

'The two girls.'

'*What?*' He stared back at her. 'Who are you talking of, Nefertiti?'

'The girls, Isikara and the maid from Naharin, must be blinded!'

'*Why?*'

'True perfume makers can only be sure of their sense of smell if not distracted by other senses. The best perfume makers are always blind. Your mother always said this!'

Amenhotep shook his head. Over the roar of the crowds, his voice was harsh. 'You have enough blind perfume makers. And Intef is the best in the world. This isn't necessary. You're going too far.'

She smiled back at him. '*I'm* not to blame that the two girls were made perfume makers. It was *you* who put them to work in the Unguent Rooms in the first place.'

CHAPTER TWENTY-FIVE

TRUTH BY THE FEATHER OF MAAT

The gardeners who delivered the rose petals wouldn't meet my eye. I kept glancing at them as they offloaded their baskets, thinking they might have news of Samut. But no one would return my look. Even the girls from the flower-press room slid their glances past me and started whispering with their heads bent low as they spread the petals on the drying tables, so I couldn't catch a word of what was said. When one of them looked up at me I thought she was about to speak, but Intef came by and she busied herself again.

I felt an uncomfortable prickle run through me. As if something was about to happen. Were they hiding something? Then before we'd even strained the jars from the previous day's steeping, I heard the sound of raised voices in the courtyard and my body turned to stone.

What if Nefertiti had decided? What if we were both being fetched right now?

As if in answer, a man strode into the room and grabbed my arms. I shrugged him away. 'Let go of me!' The room was completely silent now, with not a sound from the girls as they watched.

I stood with my back against the wall.

'What? What's happening? Why're you so silent? Say something!' I stared around at their faces. Those who met my eyes looked terrified and then looked quickly away again.

The man jerked my arms behind my back. 'Don't delay! I'm under orders to fetch you.' Across the room my eyes met the eyes of the girl who'd first warned me. She'd said it would be Isikara. She'd said nothing of me being blinded. My hands reached out to her as the man dragged me across the room.

I squinted as I was brought from the darkness into the sunshine of the courtyard. My head was swimming. Concentrate, I kept urging myself. This is the last day you'll see sunlight, and rose petals in shades from darkest red to the most delicate orange and palest pink barely tinged with colour and . . . and

... my head was spinning. Print the colours and textures on your mind *forever*, I urged myself. Soak up everything like the desert soaks up dew. And pray to Hathor that you'll never let them be lost from your head. From now onwards there will always be darkness.

Despite the heat, I was shaking uncontrollably. My legs wanted to give way. My eyes grew wide as I saw them holding Isikara and even wider when I saw Kiya. What was she doing here?

'Stay away, Kiya,' I shouted. But the guard shook me and pushed me forward. I beat against his chest and stumbled so that Kiya reached out a hand to steady me.

'Don't worry,' she whispered. 'They won't hurt you. You have to speak out.'

Won't hurt me? What was she saying? I stared back at her.

'Just tell the truth,' she whispered. 'Save yourself. Tell that Samut gave you the ring and not Tuthmosis.'

'Tell *who*?'

'Amenhotep. I've pleaded with him. If you admit it was Samut neither you nor Isikara will be blinded.'

'Isikara has nothing to do with Samut!'

'Wosret has convinced Nefertiti you were both involved in the tomb robbing. And you both helped

234

Tuthmosis escape. So you must both be punished. All you have to do is speak the truth.'

I felt the blood drain from my face. Then it all came seething back again so that my skin seemed to pulse with heat. I swallowed and tried to protest. But no words came. Surely Kiya would know this was impossible. I couldn't speak out against Samut. Yet how could I allow Isikara to be blinded?

And now they were fetching us both and Nefertiti was demanding, *Speak or I will blind you both!*

If I could only summon the strength of the seventeenth lion and roar in her face. Across the courtyard I saw Isikara watching me. Who would they take first? And what . . .? A shudder ran through me. It didn't bear thinking about. Too late. The guards had hold of her and we were both being pushed forward towards the gate. I felt my feet slide over the gravel and my legs go lame.

Kiya nodded curtly at the guards. 'Release them both! They're in my care now. I'll take them to the Great Hall.'

The guard scowled at her. 'We were told to accompany you.'

'Well, accompany us, then, but don't hold them so brutally. They're not trussed goats being led to slaughter, but women.'

'Prisoners, no less!'

'They won't be prisoners after the King has heard what they have to say.'

I glanced at her. This was a new Kiya.

A sneer swept over the guard's face. 'How can you be so sure?'

'Do as I say. Release them!'

Isikara turned. 'Wait! There is something I must fetch.' She was gone only for a few moments and then we were on our way with the guards begrudgingly following at a distance.

I looked at Kiya and forced myself to speak. 'So . . . we're truly to be blinded?'

She glanced at me in surprise. 'You have a choice. You surely won't remain silent? You can't, Ta-Miu! Be brave now. Remember how, on our journey from Mitanni to Egypt, when I was scared you kept telling me don't fear tomorrow while today's sun is still in the sky?'

But as we got to the huge cedar doors that were swung open by attendants, I felt myself falter. Not only Amenhotep but also Nefertiti sat waiting on the golden thrones, wearing the tall red crowns of Upper Egypt, while Nefertiti's cheetahs prowled restlessly around the room, their tails swinging heavily and their claws *tic-ticking* against the tiles. And standing alongside their thrones swathed in his snarling leopard-skin cloak, was Wosret.

I heard Isikara's quick intake of breath. She gripped my hand and when I turned to her, I could see the dread in her eyes. 'This is the first time I've seen Wosret since we left Thebes. May Sekhmet protect us! If Wosret's to decide our fate, I'm done for!' she whispered.

I looked back at her. 'It's not Wosret. It's me who has to decide!' There was no time for more as Kiya urged me forward.

'Speak the truth now, Ta-Miu. All you have to do is tell them it was *Samut* who broke into the tomb.'

Samut? My breath caught at the sound of his name. But before I could falter I pushed all thoughts of him away. Isikara could not be blinded because of me. Samut had betrayed me. Yes. My decision was made. I had to speak out against Samut. I nodded and heard my words come out, strange and hollow, from the back of my throat. 'I'll speak.'

Amenhotep held up his hand. 'Wait.' He beckoned to a scribe to start recording the proceedings and then for an attendant to step forward. The attendant held out a long white ostrich plume. 'Lay your hand on this and swear that you speak the truth.'

I bowed and touched the plume. My fingers were

237

shaking so much they made the fronds of the feather shiver. 'By the feather of Maat, I do.'

'Promise all you say can be recorded and forever upheld as the truth on this matter from now onwards.'

'I do!'

'Then proceed.'

I felt Kiya and Isikara standing on either side of me as I began the story of how I'd first met Samut and how I'd told him about the duplicate ankh key which opened the lock on the gate of the secret passageway that led into the Great King Amenhotep's burial chamber.

At first the words caught in my throat but eventually my voice got stronger and stronger. And as my story grew, I sensed the quietness in the Great Hall as they listened, silent as mice before the stare of a cat.

And so I damned Samut and damned myself and there was only the sound of my voice, hoarse now, as I spoke the last words, 'Isikara should not be blinded! She has suffered more than is needed. You tell the rest, Isikara. Tell of why Tuthmosis went to Nubia and who you were fleeing from and what happened in the war between Egypt and Nubia and how you came to lose your bow fingers.'

Wosret took a sudden step forward. His hand sliced through the air. '*Enough!* Enough story-telling and rambling on.' His face was flushed as he glared directly at Isikara, daring her to defy him. 'There's no need for more *trivial* confessions.'

He nodded towards Nefertiti. 'I recommend a reprieve. Let them both be freed. We've heard the maid's story. We don't need further explanations. She's accused someone by the name of Samut. That's enough evidence. He must be found immediately and punished. There's no need for further unravelling. What's needed now is quick action. The thief must be brought to trial immediately.'

Isikara tossed her head. Her eyes glinted dangerously as she edged her way past Wosret. She bowed before Amenhotep. 'There *is* need for further unravelling. Ta-Miu's story is not the whole story. You've not heard *my* side.'

'I said, *enough!* Be silent, girl! You were not asked to speak!' Wosret glowered at Isikara as if he wished his glance would pierce her heart. 'There's no need to repeat evidence, especially when it's untrue.'

Amenhotep held up his hand. 'Wait, Wosret. This girl speaks with conviction. She's the daughter of Henuka, who was the priest at the Temple of Sobek. Would the daughter of a priest lie?'

Wosret gave Amenhotep a look as if there was much he didn't know. Then he bowed low and abruptly changed his voice to a smooth tone that was like honey dripping over cake. 'She'd not *purposefully* tell lies. But she's been living a rough life amongst men in army camps. She's hardly the sort of person you can trust to speak the truth! Her brother is no better than a mercenary. He's an Egyptian paid by the Nubians to fight *against* Egypt. And in the desert, along with a girl of very dubious origins, she and Tuthmosis all took up arms against Egypt.'

Isikara swung back to face him so suddenly that one of the cheetahs snarled at her. 'The girl you speak of was enslaved by desert Medjay. Their ruthless leader could've killed her and no one would have helped her. Least of all *your* Egyptian army. Because you paid the Medjay leader to be your spy. And *you*—'

'Enough!'

Isikara spoke all the louder. '*You* would've paid him to see both Tuthmosis and I killed but we escaped!'

'What proof have you?'

'This!' Isikara turned towards Amenhotep, holding up a thick bundle of papyrus that she had grabbed from her girdle bag. 'Intef hid this for me in the Chamber of Secrets with his scrolls. It's all written here. I kept a record of everything that happened on our journey to Nubia and back. It begins with the words: *Without two fingers it is hard to grip a reed stylus.*

I wrote with difficulty because of Wosret's soldiers. They took off my fingers to prevent me from using a bow. But had I not been able to find soot for ink, I'd have written even with my own blood to set down the story of how Tuthmosis and I were pursued and captured.'

Amenhotep stood up. 'Is this true, Wosret?'

'*Lies*, my Lord! All lies! The desert has done nothing to change this girl's ill manners. When last we met she defiled your mother's embalming chamber by spitting at me!'

Isikara tossed her head. 'I would spit at you again were we not in the Great Hall before the King and Queen.'

Wosret turned his back abruptly on Isikara. He raised his arms and waved them in front of Amenhotep and Nefertiti as if gathering energy from the air. 'You can see for yourselves, the girl is deranged. You can't believe her testimony! It's all lies. She should be imprisoned *forever* for speaking such outrageous treason against *me*, the Highest of High Priests. Why would I plot to kill the future King of Egypt?'

But Isikara was not to be stopped. 'Not only did Wosret try to poison Tuthmosis, he also killed my father.'

Wosret swirled around to face her so quickly that the claws of his leopard cloak snatched at the air. 'You have *no* proof I killed your father. He died of grief when he was embalming Queen Tiy. And what possible reason would I have to poison Tuthmosis? I was his trusted mentor.'

Amenhotep spoke quietly. 'The trust was misplaced.'

Wosret glared back at him. 'You can't *possibly* believe this girl's story against mine.'

'I might not have, but I've received a similar account in a message from my brother.'

Nefertiti looked startled. 'Your *brother*? Tuthmosis has written to you? What did he say? Does he want to take the throne from you?'

'What my brother has written is a private matter between us. And will soon be resolved.'

PART FOUR

CHAPTER TWENTY-SIX

ACROSS THE RIVER

'I've found the message, my Lady.' Sitra bowed and withdrew some scraps from her girdle bag. 'But I'm afraid the papyrus has been torn into shreds. It's hard to decipher the writing.'

Nefertiti reached out. 'So you've tried to read it already, Sitra!'

'I wanted to check it was in fact a letter for your husband.'

'Silly Sitra! I'm not chastising you. I'm joking. I trust you with my heart. And I'm delighted you found it. You're cleverer than Wosret. He vows he searched everywhere and found no trace of the letter.'

Sitra shook her head. 'I don't think he could've.

I found it scattered in bits in the rose garden near his quarters.'

'That's odd. Do you think Wosret found it and tore it up?'

Sitra shrugged. 'Who can tell? But it's not what you were expecting.'

'What do you mean?'

'It's not written by Princess Tadukhepa.'

'Who wrote it, then?'

'It has Tuthmosis's cartouche. It must be from him.'

'*Tuthmosis?* Then this is the letter Amenhotep spoke of. So it's true! The message isn't from that little desert fox. But what does it say? Lay it out quickly. Can we put the pieces together and see what he's plotting?' Nefertiti ruffled through the bits of papyrus. 'Does this black flourish belong to this torn piece, or to that? And is this squiggle part of this word, or that one? We have to be clever. It's like a puzzle, Sitra.'

'Look, my Lady. Right above Tuthmosis's cartouche there's a time given. If you take this piece and join it with that one, he asks your husband to meet him.'

Nefertiti peered across Sitra's shoulder. 'Meet him? Where and why?'

'I'm not sure.'

'It's too risky for Amenhotep to meet with Tuthmosis.'

'Why?'

'It could be a trap.'

Sitra's eyebrows shot up. 'A trap?'

'Why is the message so secret? Why doesn't Tuthmosis come directly to the Palace and have a proper meeting with his brother? Why this secrecy? It can only be because Tuthmosis plans to get Amenhotep to hand over his throne.' She suddenly gripped the armrests of her chair. 'Or . . . maybe he plans to *capture* him.'

'You don't *know* this for sure, my Lady.'

'I must warn Amenhotep how dangerous it could be to meet with Tuthmosis.'

Sitra looked back at her in silence. Nefertiti could see what she was thinking. If her own position as Queen was in jeopardy, then so was Sitra's as her lady-in-waiting.

'Shouldn't you speak to Wosret first?'

She shook her head. 'After hearing the accusations against him today, I'm not sure I trust Wosret. Let's find the missing pieces of the papyrus and see if we can discover where the meeting is going to take place.'

'A word here says lake.'

'Queen Tiy's lake? Why would Tuthmosis meet

Amenhotep inside the Palace grounds if he wanted the meeting kept secret? It doesn't make sense. It would be too risky.'

'If you put this piece next to the other it makes the words "sacred lake".'

'Sitra, you're so clever! The Sacred Lake next to the Temple of Amun is where they'll meet! You deserve five gold menat necklaces as a gift. I'll have them engraved to say what a valuable person you are!'

Sitra looked alarmed instead of pleased. 'You must warn Amenhotep not to go.'

Nefertiti shook her head. 'Amenhotep loves his brother. He'll never believe me. I won't be able to prevent him going.'

'So what *will* you do?'

'Go secretly to the lake at the appointed time.'

'*What?* How will that help? Rather tell the King you'll accompany him.'

'He'll never agree.'

'But a girl alone across the river late at night . . . in your condition? What help would you be?'

'I'll hide and listen and confront Tuthmosis if I'm suspicious.'

'You *can't* go alone. Take bodyguards, at least.'

'Don't be foolish, Sitra. With an escort of guards I might as well have cymbals and drums announcing my arrival. No. It *has* to be secret. You must arrange a boat for me with a boatman who swears to silence.'

'Please don't go alone, I beg you. I'll go with you.'

'I prefer to be on my own. A dagger will be my protection.'

The night was dark and silent with a thick heavy mist that had settled over the river and muted everything. Down at the quayside the only sound came from the rhythmic slap of water against the wooden pylons. Even the frogs were silent.

'Where's the boatman, Sitra? I thought you said you'd arranged everything,' Nefertiti whispered urgently. 'A pestilence! Why does it have to be misty tonight of all nights? Can you see anything?'

'Don't fret. He'll come. I promised him enough gold.'

Nefertiti searched the darkness with the mist drifting against her face like bits of torn rag. She could barely see across to the other bank. Why couldn't Tuthmosis and Amenhotep just have met on this side? It would've been so much easier.

Sitra shuddered.

Nefertiti gave her a sharp, impatient look. 'What's the matter now?'

'I don't like to be so close to the river at night. There could be crocodiles.'

'Then you shouldn't have come. And I wish you hadn't made me wear this scratchy peasant tunic.'

'You mustn't be recognised.'

'Look! There!' Nefertiti pointed and whispered, 'See. Around that bend on this side, close to the reeds, there's a shape coming this way. Is it a boat?'

'Praise Horus, let it be!' Sitra let out a sigh.

The dark, upturned prow of a boat loomed through the mist. The man rowing it had thrown a cloak about his shoulders and head so he was hardly distinguishable from the shape of the boat itself. There was no flare burning in the prow but as he came alongside the quay, he held up a small oil lamp that must have been hidden at his feet. His features were indistinct under the cloth that covered his head.

'I was delayed.' His voice had the roughness of a throat used to quaffing strong wine. 'There were other boats out on the river. I had to keep to the shadows of the bank.'

'Probably Tuthmosis and Amenhotep, both making their separate crossings,' Sitra whispered.

'There's no time to tie up. Hurry now. Step into the boat. I can't hold it forever alongside the quay in this current,' he said brusquely, without extending a hand to help Nefertiti. It was clear the man had no idea of who she was.

He edged the boat quickly away from the quay. The Great River ran silently beneath them as he dipped his oars into the dark, syrupy surface. Then somewhere out in the middle of the river the mist suddenly evaporated and the water turned to silver with the moonlight catching and shattering against each ripple. A black sky, heavy with stars, opened above them. In the boat all three were silent. Now they were out in the main stream in full view of anyone who might be watching.

Across on the opposite bank Nefertiti saw the first gateway of the Temple looming up through the darkness with a few final shreds of mist at its base. The eastern bank was devoid of light. Much darker than she'd expected. Surely there should have been flares burning somewhere to light the way? She'd never been out alone at night without attendants and a lighted path to guide her every step. Now the cool breeze wafting over the river made her shiver as the boat bumped with a dull thud against the landing quay.

'Stay here in the boat,' she whispered to Sitra. 'I'm going alone.' She patted the dagger that hung from her waist concealed by the folds of her tunic. 'I have this to protect me.'

'But—'

'I'm *ordering* you, Sitra! If you don't stay, the boatman might not wait for me.'

As she stepped onto the ramp Nefertiti saw that the paving had not been swept since the celebration of Gempaaten. The entire walkway was still strewn with bits and pieces dropped by the crowd. Squashed food. Horse droppings. A shred of ribbon. A broken rush sandal. Left lying just as they had been dropped.

She thought of the sunlight and the crowds and the light reflecting off the gold and silvered chariots. Could it have been only a day before? Now the long walkway stretching ahead in the moonlight between the shadowed faces of the ram-headed sphinxes seemed strange and daunting. She walked slowly at first, aware of being totally alone and yet at the same time sensing the unblinking eyes of the sphinxes staring at her from either side of the walkway, every now and again glancing back over her shoulder in case someone was following, her footsteps getting faster and faster and echoing against the paving, until she was almost running.

What if she was wrong? What if she had misunderstood the message? What if Tuthmosis had something else in mind? All this secrecy . . . what was it for? Then a thought suddenly hit her and stopped her as sharply as if someone had pulled her back with reins.

If Tuthmosis wanted to capture Amenhotep he would have planned it differently.

There was only one explanation for this secrecy – a *murder*!

Tuthmosis planned to *murder* Amenhotep!

As if in answer to this thought, she caught a movement from the corner of her eye. A shadow dropped from a stone wall, dark, swift, silent, and disappeared into a pool of darkness. It *had* to be Tuthmosis. Who else would be creeping about so stealthily? Surely not Amenhotep?

She shrank back against a pillar. As she stood watching and waiting, the shadow emerged again and paused on the palely lit steps, then disappeared between the pillars into the vast space beyond, where the darkness of the Temple of Amun turned into a deep, cavernous void. Now the steps where only the day before at the celebration of Gempaaten Wosret had stood waiting, were empty.

There was only one option. If she wanted to reach the Sacred Lake within the walled complex, she'd have to enter the Temple and follow the sound of the footfalls through the darkness.

CHAPTER TWENTY-SEVEN

THE SACRED LAKE

Nefertiti was just a few paces inside the Temple with its row upon row of massive columns, when she realised it was hopeless. The slight glimmer of moonlight coming in from the doorway soon dissolved in thick darkness. And the light entering far above through small openings at ceiling height barely reached through the forest of pillars.

The person might be anywhere in the darkness. Right now he could be standing only a few paces away, observing her. Perhaps even as close as the nearest column.

A shiver passed down her spine. Why hadn't she insisted that Sitra accompany her? Then the sound of breathing made her heart leap like a flame caught in a draught. She stood silent as a stone pillar, not daring to take a breath herself. The person was close. So close that maybe a hand would touch her.

But who? Tuthmosis or Amenhotep? Even if she had tried to say a name, she couldn't have. Her throat had closed. She couldn't utter a sound.

Then the soft swish of rush sandals against stone. The person was walking away. She waited until the sound disappeared. There was only one option. It was safer to cling to the side walls instead of following directly through the dark space of the Temple. With her fingers searching for the smooth stone, she groped her way to the southern side door that led out to the Sacred Lake.

Who would she find waiting there? Tuthmosis or Amenhotep?

As she came out into the open, the silvery surface of the lake appeared like a huge expanse of cracked glass in the moonlight. She slunk forward into a shadow cast by a pillar and stood with her back flattened against its stone. What if someone was watching her from the walls? Her throat tightened. Now she longed for the mist to come back down again and hide her.

The moonlight and shadows were playing tricks on her. Every rustle, every movement seemed like a person. She narrowed her eyes to focus. Yes, someone was already standing alongside the huge carved scarab beetle at the edge of the moon-splintered lake.

Tuthmosis or Amenhotep? It was hard to tell from such a distance. If it was Amenhotep, she should go forward and warn him. But what if she got there and found herself face to face with Tuthmosis?

He has a sense of foreboding. As if at any moment something will loom up out of the shadows next to him. The darkness and the sounds of the night, the rustlings, squeaks and sighs that sough through the air have set his imagination running. He feels the hair on his arms prickle and his heart quicken.

An owl swoops down. The sharp cry of its prey ends in a strangled screech. An uneasy silence follows.

Who's there? He wants to call out. But there is nothing except the hoarse bark of a dog coming from a distance and the sharp, dry smell of dust and a more pungent smell that pinches his nose. Perhaps a desert fox, prowling for scraps of food at the offering altars.

He glances about uneasily, his eyes running slowly over his surroundings.

The towering statue of his father glares down from his pedestal, the stony eyes narrowed and unblinking, the edges of his gigantic nostrils flaring, the carved line of his lips sneering. Behind the statue, the Temple of

Amun is silent and secretive, its pillars and stones sliced into blocks of light and shade by the bloodless moon. Creatures etched into the stone walls – curved claws, jagged snouts, fierce fangs – are frozen into silence. And throats and chests of enemies are forever stilled as they wait for the arrows directed at their hearts.

His fingers rest on the sculpture of the giant scarab beetle polished with the touch of so many hands. Here, beside the moon-splintered lake, he feels trapped. This is the wrong place to have agreed to meet his brother. The Inner Sanctum might have been safer. In the Inner Sanctum the spirit of the gods would surely protect the son of a king against the dark evils of the night.

But already it is too late. An imperceptible movement makes him turn. The merest flicker. But still a movement. He sees the half-expected figure. The face made pale by the moonlight. The object that glints.

Nefertiti caught sight of the shadow again. It was slinking forward and creeping stealthily towards the figure standing at the lake. Why would Amenhotep steal up like this? It was surely not him. It had to be Tuthmosis sneaking up on Amenhotep already standing there.

Now she had to act. She had to warn Amenhotep. She crouched low, felt for the dagger still concealed below her tunic and drew it slowly out of its sheath. 'Sekhmet fill me with your lion spirit. Be beside me tonight.'

The hardness of the ivory handle in her hand and the sharpness of the double-sided blade as she ran her thumb over it made her strength return. Clutching it tightly, she crept forward.

Now the silhouettes of the two men were sharply outlined against the silvered water but it was impossible to know which was Amenhotep and which Tuthmosis.

Then an object glinted in the moonlight. The quickest flash of light. Then a single utterance like an explosion of breath. An anguished choke rather than a cry for help. 'You!' The single word escaped into the night.

Whose throat?

Nefertiti sprang forward but she was too late. The glinting object disappeared into the folds of a person. He staggered. Then slowly dropped to his knees and crumpled at her feet.

'Amenhotep!' Her voice echoed against the stone walls. She heard the sound of it rise up, the breeze blowing it like a flapping pennant out over the water

of the lake. 'Amenhotep! Amenhotep . . .!' She dropped down beside him and clutched his shoulders,
wrapping him in her arms. 'Amenhotep!'

Vaguely she sensed the shape of the man next to
her. Then a breathless voice right up close. 'Nefertiti.
I'm here! I'm here beside you!'

'*Amenhotep?*' She flung her head back to stare up at
him. Then looked back at the person she was cradling
in her arms. 'But . . .?'

Amenhotep was staring down at her. 'You've blood
on your hands! Are you injured? What has he done to
you?' He grabbed hold of her. Then pulled back
sharply as he suddenly saw the figure lying on the
ground and looked back at what she was still clutching. '*What?* A dagger? Nefertiti what have you *done?*'

'*Done?* I've done nothing! It was *you*, Amenhotep! I
saw you plunge the dagger into him! But the darkness
muddled me. I didn't know who was who. I thought
he had killed *you!*'

'Me? I've just come.' He bent down quickly and
lifted the shoulders of the man lying on the ground.

The arms fell limply back but the face made pale by
the moonlight was that of Tuthmosis.

'*Tuthmosis!*' Amenhotep spun around to face her.
'Nefertiti, may the gods deliver us. What have you
done? You've killed my brother!'

'Me?' She stepped back. 'It was *you* who killed him! I thought the person who plunged the dagger was Tuthmosis and it was *you* lying here on the ground. *You* that Tuthmosis had killed. Then I turned and found you at my side. So it was the other way around. *You* killed him! It was *your* dagger!'

Amenhotep stooped and cradled the body of Tuthmosis against him and pressed his hand hard against the wound in his chest. But in the moonlight Nefertiti saw the blood run freely and gather quickly, darkly and almost black in a pool on the paving beneath him. And when Amenhotep held his cheek against the face, she knew he'd feel no breath.

Amenhotep flung his head back and stared at her, his eyes like glassy stones glittering in the moonlight. 'Tuthmosis came to make peace, not war! Why have you done this?'

'Me? It wasn't *my* dagger that killed him!' Her words seemed pulled from the base of her throat. 'My blade is clean. I swear! I came here to protect you.'

Amenhotep jumped up and took her by the shoulders and shook her. 'If not yours, whose dagger then? *Whose* work is this? Tell me! *Who* was the person you brought with you to do this terrible thing? Tell me!'

Nefertiti pushed him away from her. 'I brought no

other person. I was alone. I left my maid at the boat with the boatman.'

'But there was a third person here. Didn't you see? I thought he'd injured you.'

'What person? It was dark.'

Amenhotep swung around and stared over his shoulder. 'Didn't you see him when you were crouching down? He ran past me as I arrived.'

'You're not making sense.'

'Someone ran swiftly past me.'

'Then it was *that* person who killed Tuthmosis.'

CHAPTER TWENTY-EIGHT

THE FUNERARY BARGE

Isikara felt her jaw clench as the cortège began its slow movement from the steps of the Temple of Amun through the avenue of sphinxes to the quayside.

The procession walked in absolute silence. The sombre, hushed movement of people had muted even the children and city dogs. Alongside the bank the funerary barge, unpainted and strewn with lilies and lotus flowers, was waiting to take the body upstream to be blessed at the Southern Opet Temple before transporting it to the Wabet chamber for embalming.

So silent. How could a procession of so many people be so utterly quiet?

Far ahead beyond the bobbing clay-covered heads of the priests, Isikara caught sight of the brilliant splashes of red that were the tall plumes in the crowns of Amenhotep and Nefertiti as they led the procession in separate carrying chairs of ebony and gold set with precious stones that glinted in the sunlight.

Isikara herself had been called upon to hurriedly dye the white plumes red, to mark a time of mourning. She'd used the alkanet dye from a recipe she'd devised in Nubia. In the desert she had dyed feathers for the arrows of her brother Katep, and her friend Anoukhet. And also for Tuthmosis.

Now she could barely breathe his name.

The feathers she'd gathered for Tuthmosis's arrows she'd dyed blue to mark his royal birth. A colour worthy of someone who should have worn the blue Khepresh Warrior Crown. The prince who should have been King.

Now her hands were stained red with alkanet from Nefertiti's and Amenhotep's ostrich plumes. Red, as if stained with Tuthmosis's very own blood. And even though she'd washed and washed her hands as if in the washing she could scrub away the horrible deed, the red had remained to remind her that someone else's hands were stained too. But with Tuthmosis's life-blood.

Tuthmosis had been murdered. But by whom? *Who* had wished him dead? Wosret? Amenhotep? Nefertiti?

Perhaps even Nefertiti's maid? Rumour had it they'd all been at the Sacred Lake. And the gods knew they each had reason. But which one of them had plunged the dagger into his chest?

In the early dawn even before the Sky Goddess, Nut, had plucked the golden orb of the sun from the east, the news had spread. And in the sleeping city of Thebes people woke as screams of anguish reverberated across the Great River to be replaced by soft wails of mourning and the hollow rattling of sistrums. Women throughout the city had raised their arms in sorrow and the men of Thebes had sunk slowly to their knees and begun sprinkling dust over their heads and tying white bands around their foreheads as dawn broke red as a bloodstain.

Her own throat had been too tight and raw to utter a single sound. She had returned to the familiarity of the Unguent Rooms. There, in the quiet of the courtyard, her hands had worked numbly, steeping the feathers in the red liquid. She had hung them to dry in the hot wind that had sprung up from the desert at sunrise, while Intef stood silently by . . . his presence holding a comfort more than words.

Now, as the cortège moved forward, a heat haze was gathering far in the distance in the tomb-riddled landscape of the Theban hills with their entrances

264

facing east so the rising sun would wake the dead from their sleep. But Tuthmosis would never be woken. Not in this world. When he went to meet Maat and Thoth at the weighing scales, his heart would be found light but not light enough to *ever* return to her in Thebes.

Hathor, Lady of the West, had stolen him forever.

The early morning shadows of the sphinxes cast long stripes across the procession as it shuffled forward. The sun had gained strength and the smell of myrrh and incense from the smoking censers that priests were swinging made the air even hotter. Isikara felt the sand chafing between her toes and sandals and was grateful for the wind that blew through her robes bringing some relief.

Through a gap in the crowd she saw past the priests and female mourners and suddenly caught sight of the body carried by bearers on its lion-pawed bier. Two falcon-headed priestesses walked alongside, one at the head, the other at the foot of the bier. Just as the goddesses Isis and Nepthys had done with their brother, Osiris.

Isikara longed to be up close to Tuthmosis. From where she was, so far back in the procession, she couldn't see his face. It was impossible to believe that he, her constant companion since before the time of the previous flood of the Great River, lay dead on that bier.

It was impossible to believe Tuthmosis was *truly* dead.

The first time she'd seen him lying in his leopard cloak on the stone bed in the Wabet chamber, she'd thought him dead. Wosret had poisoned him and was waiting for him to die. But her father had saved him.

Wosret! She could hardly bear to think of him.

The bier was eventually set down at the quay with the red plumes of Nefertiti and Amenhotep drawing everyone's eyes towards it. Now the procession broke up and people began proceeding to the various flower-lined barges alongside the quay. Isikara glanced quickly at Ta-Miu and Kiya and signalled with her eyes that she would only be a moment. Then she pushed ahead to catch one final glimpse of Tuthmosis.

He lay with his piercing blue eyes closed, his lips quiet, his hair dressed in a short Nubian wig and his chest covered by a jewelled collar. On top of this lay a human-headed bird with golden wings spread protectively over his chest . . . an amulet representing his fluttering soul hovering above him. The outstretched wings studded with precious stones masked any sign of a wound or any place that had once been covered by blood.

The two falcon-headed priestesses were enticing his soul to return to his body. 'Come for my soul, O guardians of the heavens! May it rest in my body so that it will never be destroyed,' they called.

This is what every Theban believed. That the soul would return to the body.

But *she* couldn't believe it! How could any soul come back into those closed eyes and light them up again for her? Tuthmosis was dead and dead he would remain. When she saw him again after seventy days at his final funeral procession, his face would be wrapped in layers and layers of linen and lie hidden behind a golden mummy mask sealed within a mummy case, and oxen would draw his sledge into the Theban hills with musicians going before him and dancers waiting at the entrance to his tomb.

Finally the mummy case would remain behind in the burial chamber, silent and alone in the darkness, and the tomb would be sealed closed.

Now she shuddered as the drummer began a slow drumbeat. No experience as an embalmer had prepared her for this moment when Tuthmosis's body was lifted on the bier and placed in the flower-strewn barge to begin this journey.

She cast a last look at his silent face.

All around her the women mourners set up their

desolate cries. Along the riverbanks people bowed their dust-strewn heads to their knees and children scattered lotus flowers that perfumed the air and floated on the water in its path as the barge sailed by, while the slow dip of the oars joined the women's dreadful lament.

CHAPTER TWENTY-NINE

OUTSIDE THE TEMPLE OF OPET

In the jostling crowds I lost sight of Isikara and gripped Kiya's arm as we were pushed along by mourners and women rattling sistrums in our faces.

It was hot beyond words. A thick, billowing cloud of yellow dust was sweeping in from the desert and clouding the sky with smokiness. I felt the dust scouring my eyes and throat and swept a hand across my face to brush away the sand sticking to it. Today the loaves of unleavened bread for mourning would be sprinkled not just with flour, but with the grit of Egypt.

By the time the barge had reached the quay at the Southern Temple of Opet, I caught sight of Isikara again and edged my way towards her. A shadow seemed to have settled on her face and her eyes were red-rimmed, not just from the sand.

'Are you all right?' My voice sounded shaky and not my own.

Isikara nodded as she ducked her head and pulled a linen veil across her forehead to keep out the dust. 'Well enough.'

'You shouldn't have come. You should've stayed behind to grieve in peace. Don't follow the procession into the Temple. Wait here with Kiya. I'll bring you both something to drink. Stay here close to the statue of Hathor. I'll see what I can find.'

I hurried through the crowds, hoping to see someone selling pomegranate juice.

'There she is!' I heard a voice from somewhere behind me as I shouldered my way through the people. 'It's that moonstruck girl. Haven't seen *her* in a while.'

I recognised the voice. It was one of the old sweeping ladies from the Temple. I tried to twist around to catch sight of her but the crowd pushed me on.

'They say she's been in prison.'

'Hmmph! Prison hasn't done much for her looks. Look how scraggy she is. There'll be no boys running after her until she puts some flesh on those bones.'

'And you should know, Meryt! You've got enough flesh to entice ten boys! You'd have to spend a lifetime in prison to lose all the flesh from *your* bones.'

'A frog in your mouth, Senen! May your jowls hang down to your breasts one of these days.'

'I've seen no sign of her lazy boyfriend lately. They say . . .'

The voices were trailing off. *They say* what? I wanted to ask. Did they have news of Samut? I twisted around trying to see the direction they'd taken but the throng was so tightly packed, I was pushed along no matter and it was all I could do to stay upright without my feet stumbling along beneath me.

Suddenly a voice hissed next to my ear. 'Traitor!'

I turned swiftly and nearly fell. Then felt a strong grip on my arm, not so much to keep me from falling, as to inflict pain.

'Let go of me!' I yelled and tried to fling off the hand, then looked up straight into the eyes of Samut.

'*Samut!* Samut, where have you been?' Without thinking I thumped my fists into his chest. 'Why didn't you come for me?'

He wrenched my fists away. 'Get away from me!'

'What? What have *I* done? I've been in prison all this time. You should have come to have me freed. Why didn't you?' I hammered at him again.

He grabbed my hands and flung them away. 'Don't touch me, traitor!'

'What are you talking of? Have you gone mad? You left me in prison. Where have you *been*? They said you were to be arrested.' I stared into his dark eyes but saw no spark of warmth in them.

'I'm still free, as you can see! But not because of you!' A small muscle twitched at the side of his jaw. 'You know what I'm talking about. You betrayed me.' He turned away abruptly.

'Wait!' I grabbed hold of his arm and drew him urgently back. 'You can't leave. Listen! I didn't purposely betray you! You *must* believe me. All the time while I waited for you to come to me in prison, I kept silent. I spoke out only when they announced Isikara would be blinded. All I did was speak the truth. I told them you'd given me the ring. I said no more than that. You *must* understand.'

'What treachery! You told them I knew about the key.'

'But I didn't say you *used* the key. You must understand I was forced to speak out.'

'I do understand. You're nothing but a hussy!'

'*What?*'

He glared back at me. 'Tuthmosis was more important to you. All the time you pretended to love me, you were thinking only of him. And then the moment he returned you betrayed me, hoping he'd come rushing to your side. Well he hasn't, has he?'

'I *never* betrayed you! I never said you entered the tomb. How could I? I didn't know for sure. And why do you speak like this about Tuthmosis when he has been murdered and right now they are taking his body to the Temple? May Horus protect you.' I quickly drew a wedjat eye in the sand with the toe of my sandal. 'Have you no respect?'

'*Respect!*' Samut hissed. 'For someone like Tuthmosis! You ask about respect? What respect did you have for *me* when you betrayed me?'

'It wasn't a betrayal. And it's different to having respect for someone of Royalty who's been murdered.'

'Royalty!' He spat at the ground. 'What respect should I have for Royalty, with their churlish manners and disdainful ways, behaving as if they are gods?'

'Tuthmosis wasn't churlish! His only fault was that he was born rich.'

'Hah! Protect him as much as you like. But neither he, nor his father, showed *me* any respect.'

'*You?* What were you to them?'

'What do you care?'

I eyed him. This hard, glowering face was one I didn't know. 'You're jealous.'

'Jealous? Of their wealth? Or do you think I'm jealous because you loved him more than me? Well I'm *not*! If it was Tuthmosis you wanted then so be it! With every breath in my body I hated him!'

'Hated? You don't know what you're saying. How can you speak like this when he is hardly dead?'

'Hardly dead? Believe me, Tuthmosis is *very* dead.'

Samut stared at me with eyes as stony and cold and hard as black onyx. For a moment my breath caught.

He nodded. 'I know that for sure.'

'*You?* Samut . . .?' I could hardly find the words. 'What are you talking of? Did you . . .?'

'*Kill* your beloved?' he sneered. 'Do you think I'd tell you if I had? So you can run off to Amenhotep and report on me? You and your precious Kiya, the Princess Tadukhepa, who flirts with Amenhotep! You're all the same. Nefertiti as well! Flirting and carrying on, having everything your own way and still making sure that you come out of it innocent. Whores, that's what the lot of you are!'

'Samut, don't speak like that! We *are* innocent.'

'You don't think Nefertiti's innocent?'

I stared at him in disbelief. 'What are you saying? You mean *she* killed Tuthmosis?'

'Nefertiti's too clever for that! She'd never dirty her hands. She wouldn't risk her position with Amenhotep by being held responsible for his brother's death. But she's cunning. She has Wosret on her side. She stops at nothing to have her own way. She thought one little beckon from her would have me running.'

'What are you talking of?'

'She tried to flirt with me just like you and Kiya. She would have kissed me, had I let her.'

'What?'

Samut sneered. 'Surprised, aren't you? Yes. At the stables.'

'The stables? But that's where you took me. Did you take Nefertiti there as well?'

'She came after me. You don't believe me, do you?'

I stared back at him taking in every detail of his expression and the line of the lips I had once kissed and the eyes as hard as onyx that had once sparkled. My arms dropped heavily to my sides. I nodded slowly like someone in a dream. 'I do believe you. You hate us all.'

In reply an awful sneer spread across his mouth. And then it was as if the spirit of Sekhmet suddenly entered into me. I couldn't bear to have him look at

me like that. I flung myself at him, leapt at his throat
and dug my fingers into his neck.

'It *was* you, wasn't it? It was *you* who plunged the
dagger into Tuthmosis! You *murderer!*'

CHAPTER THIRTY

POISON

'Ta-Miu, where have you been?' Someone was shaking me. I stared blindly back at the girl standing in front of me, my thoughts as murky as the dust-filled air. Who was she and what was she was doing here?

And then, I realised it was Isikara. She bent down and shook me again. 'Ta-Miu? What's going on? What happened? I've been searching everywhere for you. I waited and waited but you didn't come. Kiya is frantic with worry. The procession is over. Everyone has returned to the Palace.'

Her words ran together. Sounds that had no meaning. I looked down at my hands. There was blood on them. And blood and dirt under my finger-nails. How had it got there? I squinted back at her against the sun that was already sinking behind the smoky horizon. 'What?'

She sat down on the riverbank and held my face between her hands. 'Ta-Miu, what's happened? Are you ill?'

I turned my head away so as not to meet her eyes. This was Isikara. The girl who had loved Tuthmosis. Her papyrus had said everything. I had read every single word of it. The one she had planned to show Amenhotep. She had pushed it into my hands without speaking in the early hours of this morning after we heard of Tuthmosis's murder.

She had swirled the red dye around and around in the stone basin. I had sat in a corner of the court-yard with the sky barely light and had read on and on as the stars paled and the words became clearer and clearer. Finally the very last sentence appeared, *May anyone who reads these words, know they are written by the feather of Truth, under the protection of the Eye of the Moon.*

I had sat in silence and watched the slow drip of red fall from the feathers as Isikara hung them out to dry.

She hadn't needed to speak. I knew then that she truly loved Tuthmosis. I had read it in her words. We had both loved him but she was the one more worthy of his love.

Now I couldn't meet her eyes. I twisted away from her. 'Leave me alone.'

'Ta-Miu, we are *all* mourning Tuthmosis.'

I nodded without being able to speak properly. 'Yes . . . but *I* . . .'

'You what?'

I shrugged. 'I caused his death.'

Isikara flinched. The shadow was back on her face. 'What are you saying? *You* plunged the dagger into Tuthmosis?'

I pulled at her tunic and shook my head so vigorously I felt the plaits of my wig swing against my neck. 'No! *Never!*'

'Then what?'

'*Samut* killed Tuthmosis.'

'Samut? Don't be foolish. It couldn't have been him. Why would he draw attention to himself? Samut's already on the run for having stolen the ring.'

'I saw him.'

'You *saw* him murder Tuthmosis? Why didn't you speak out before?'

'*No!* I saw him in the crowd.' I buried my head against my knees to blot out Samut's expression. The look of a wild animal. Not the Samut I knew. I spoke into the fabric of my tunic. 'He pulled me aside. He seemed demented.'

279

'Did he admit to it?'

'He rambled on about Kiya and Nefertiti and me. He said he hated Tuthmosis.'

'Because of you?'

'That's all I can believe. I attacked him then.'

'For the love of Horus, Ta-Miu, *what* did you do?' Isikara jumped up and took hold of my shoulders and shook me. 'There's blood on your hands. Have you *killed* Samut?'

I pulled away from her. 'I wish I had. I'd have throttled him for that sneer on his face. But I wasn't strong enough. He threw me off and laughed in my face. And now *you* must hate me too.'

There was a drawn-out silence while we each sifted through our own thoughts looking for the bits that made sense. Isikara stood quiet for such a long time that I turned to glance at her. She was staring out over the river watching some fishermen in reed boats throw nets into the water and plucking absently at a piece of reed. A red dragonfly touched lightly against the back of her neck like the exotic clasp of a necklace.

Suddenly she sighed as if she needed to fill her lungs with air. 'The boats seem frail, as if they could never stay afloat. But they're stronger than you think. Ours took us upstream against the current nearly all the way to the First Cataract at Syene. A long journey and an even longer one coming home from the furthest reaches of Nubia in the south all the way back to Thebes.'

I picked up a handful of pebbles and hurled them into the water. 'Don't speak like this! I know about your journey.'

'Tuthmosis came back to Thebes for a reason. To make peace.'

'I know. I can't bear this. I know how much you loved him. Don't go on.' I took hold of her hands and pulled her down beside me. 'Isikara, I beg you, listen. I know you can never forgive me but I need one last favour. Do you know the recipe for making poison?'

Isikara glanced sharply back at me. '*Poison?* Of course I do. It's intricate and complex. The exact measurements of venom have to be correct. If the mixture is too dilute, death can be slow and horrible. It's not as easy as making a mixture of fat for rubbing into the scalp to cure baldness, or making a powder of the ground skull of a catfish fried in oil, for whooping cough.' She narrowed her eyes at me. '*Who* do you plan to poison?'

'Myself.'

'What?' Her eyebrows shot high.

'It's the only way. Mix a poison but blend it

with honey and milk so my throat won't know its bitterness.'

'Why?'

'How can I live knowing Samut killed Tuthmosis because of me?'

Isikara tossed her head. 'Do you think I would mix a poison to help you die? Why should I?'

'I beg you, Isikara. I'm not brave enough to plunge a dagger into my heart, or hold a viper to my throat, or throw myself to the crocodiles. I'm not brave enough for any of these. I know you can never forgive me. But have enough pity to do this last thing.'

'You can't possibly believe Samut committed murder just because of *you!*'

'Why else?'

'He's never done anything for anyone. You heard the stories in the Unguent Rooms. He didn't even steal the ring especially for you.'

I sat back from her. 'You don't know that. You've never met him.'

'Are you defending a *murderer?* Don't be foolish, Ta-Miu. He did this for another reason. And the only one I can think of is that *Wosret* was part of this plan.'

'How?'

'Wosret wanted Tuthmosis out of the way. Tuthmosis came back to Thebes to prove his innocence and to expose Wosret. If Samut wielded the dagger when Tuthmosis died, it was *Wosret* who gave the order.'

'How can you be so sure?'

'I know Wosret better than you.' She shook her head. 'I won't make a poison. You can't kill yourself. You must tell Amenhotep and Nefertiti what Samut said.'

'I can't.'

'You *have* to! Or ask Kiya to do it for you. You've spoken out against Samut before, the second time will be easier. Do it this time for Tuthmosis.'

I knew she was right. But could I?

CHAPTER THIRTY-ONE

THE CHEETAHS

Amenhotep glanced at Kiya. 'If what you say is true, then your serving girl, this boy named Samut, Isikara and Wosret must *all* be summoned for questioning . . .'

Kiya bowed. 'By the feather of Maat, I speak the truth.'

Nefertiti narrowed her eyes. 'Why would your serving girl accuse Samut of murder?'

'Her friendship was misplaced.'

Nefertiti's eyebrow shot up in an arc. 'She has caused Tuthmosis's death by her thoughtlessness.'

Kiya looked directly back at Nefertiti. 'It's Isikara's opinion that Wosret was behind it.'

Nefertiti tossed her head so that her earrings

jangled. '*Isikara!* Why should I believe her? She has no position in Thebes.'

Amenhotep placed a hand on Nefertiti's shoulder. 'We're only calling for the truth. If Wosret played a part in Tuthmosis's murder he must be driven out of Thebes. I believe what Tuthmosis wrote in his letter. The power of the priests is too great.' He waved to his Chief Vizier. 'Call Wosret immediately, and the two girls, so that we can hear the truth. And call for a scribe to make notes of the proceedings.'

As he spoke, a slightly dishevelled-looking Wosret hurried into the hall and bowed breathlessly before Amenhotep and Nefertiti. The cheetahs, sprawled out sleeping on red cushions on the floor alongside Nefertiti, lifted their heads at the disturbance.

His eyes darted between the animals and the King and Queen. 'My Lord and Lady, I rushed to your side immediately on hearing the news.'

Amenhotep inclined his head. 'What news, Wosret?'

'The news that Samut is the murderer.'

'How can you possibly know this? We've just heard it ourselves.'

Wosret waved his arms about. 'News travels faster than dust.' Then he went on breathlessly. 'This is a grave moment. I've sent out guards once again to search for Samut. To have a murderer in our midst is *inconceivable*. Someone so evil that he would kill the brother of a King! I'm glad I'm at hand to deal with this. However, for the time being Samut can't be found.'

Amenhotep frowned. 'It's extremely odd that he's disappeared without trace.'

'Not when you're a murderer. Nor can the girls be found.'

Kiya looked up sharply. 'Isikara and Ta-Miu? But that's impossible. I left them a moment ago in my quarters.'

'And now they're gone!' Wosret shrugged and clicked his fingers as if some magic had been called upon to make them disappear so quickly. Then he bowed to Amenhotep and Nefertiti again. 'In your moment of grief neither of you are strong enough to cope with such matters. Leave it all to me. I'll have Samut found and questioned and punished. It needs someone of experience in these matters.'

Amenhotep frowned again. 'What I can't understand is why you didn't arrest Samut when we first discovered he was the tomb robber. And *are* you experienced in matters of murder?'

Wosret seemed taken by surprise. His hand stopped in mid-air. Then he quickly regained his composure. 'There were murders in Thebes when your father was King.'

'Matters of poisonings?'

'Poisonings?' He shrugged and narrowed his eyes at Amenhotep for a moment as if he wished he could click his fingers and he *too* would be gone. 'I'm not sure to what you refer. No, I mean all types of murders committed by rogues who wanted the downfall of Egypt. I, the Highest of High Priests, have sworn allegiance to Egypt and am bound to serve in the best possible way. Of this you can be assured.'

'Your best is sometimes in doubt.'

'In doubt?' Wosret's eyes darted from Amenhotep to Nefertiti. 'What do you mean? I was a mentor to your brother, Tuthmosis. May Hathor carry his soul into the West.' He bowed low. 'And a mentor to you as well. I've given loyal service to Egypt.'

'I'm suspicious of your service. I'm relieving you of some of your duties. From now onwards there'll be no more secret Inner Sanctum. Temples will be open so worship and rituals can be observed by all. Aten's light will shine in.'

'Aten? What about Amun, Mut and Khonsu? Their rituals are private. A matter between only the gods and the priests. Every day in the Inner Sanctum they are begged and placated by my priests. How else do you think we keep the God of Chaos away?'

Amenhotep shook his head. 'We've lived too long by secret rituals. From now onwards, the God of Chaos will be kept away by Aten's light. The light of the sun-disc will banish all darkness from our minds and hearts. Aten's power is greater than that of Amun or *any* of the Amun priests.'

'*What?*' Wosret flung his arms upwards. 'This is blasphemous. How can you allow commoners to observe secret rituals? And *you*, the son of a King, speak like this!'

'Not the *son* of a King. You forget Wosret, I *am* the King. Appointed by you.'

'Exactly!' Wosret spun around with his arms spread wide. 'Nefertiti . . .!' The cheetahs growled from their cushions at his sudden movement. Wosret made a slight movement to kick at the nearest one but then seemed to think better of it. 'Nefertiti, I appeal to you. Talk sense into your husband. Your child will be born into a land of chaos. If you continue with this nonsense and the gods aren't there to protect us Egypt will fall to her enemies.'

Nefertiti raised an eyebrow as dark as a kestrel's wing and shook her head. 'You forget your place, Wosret. I must listen to my husband.'

'*What?*' Wosret's mouth took on an ugly sneer. 'You've never listened to anyone. You're the most wilful person I know. And now you say you'll listen to someone who's hardly old enough to have hair sprouting on his chin?'

Wosret swung abruptly to face Amenhotep. 'And *you*? What do you say to finding your wife with a dagger in her hands over the body of your brother? If you are looking to find the *real* murderer don't look to Samut, look no further than the one who sits on the throne right beside you.'

Nefertiti leapt up so quickly that her cheetahs sprang from their cushions as well. 'You have no right!—'

'I have every right,' Wosret interrupted. 'I'm only trying to protect you *both* from scandal. None of what I say will leave this hall. I'll protect you from the scandal of the evil deed you committed.'

'*I?*' For once Nefertiti was completely at a loss for words.

Amenhotep shook his head. 'There's no scandal, Wosret. I was there. I know what happened. Nefertiti is not the murderer. Her blade was clean.'

Wosret moved in closer and took Amenhotep by the arm and spoke in a voice that dripped with honey. 'You're mistaken. Think of this. What was she doing next to the Sacred Lake so late at night? She needed no extra motivation to do the deed. She'd already confessed to me she hated Tuthmosis for returning to take your throne.' He swung around and pointed at Nefertiti. 'Ask *her*, not Samut, about Tuthmosis's death. I was ready to make Samut a scapegoat. To blame it on him for both your sakes to avoid a royal scandal. But *she* is the true murderer.'

Nefertiti's eyes glittered as hard as gemstones. 'You'll regret this!'

Amenhotep shook his head. 'You can't persuade me, Wosret. You twist things around this way and that like someone wringing out wet washing. But I read my brother's note. I believe the truth in his words. You yourself know what was written. You read the note as well.'

'Your private note? How was *I* to read it?'

'Because it disappeared from a locked chest and was found shredded near your quarters by my wife's maid. *I* certainly didn't tear it into pieces.'

'How can you be sure I read it? Do you believe her story against mine?'

'If you've sent guards out after Samut, why do you suddenly accuse my wife?'

'I told you. To prevent a scandal.'

'I don't believe your story. You're hiding the truth

behind a haze of smoke and reflection. I no longer trust you. From this day, I'm taking away your power. The temples will have Amun's name removed. The name of Aten will be carved in his place.'

'What? You can't deface the Temples, the very holiest of holy places! I *forbid* it!'

'You can't forbid it! Aten is the god of Light who has no secrecy, no hidden places. He needs no companions to do his work. I no longer have need of you or your priests of Amun.'

Suddenly Wosret made a quick gesture. He grabbed something from his girdle and lunged forward. But in a blur both cheetahs sprang and knocked him to the floor. A dagger went spinning across the hard tiles. One cheetah stood snarling with its forepaws firmly planted against Wosret's lower body, the other lay crouched against his chest, its lips pulled back in a ferocious snarl, the exposed fangs hovering at the base of Wosret's throat.

For a moment there was absolute silence as if a nest of scorpions had paralysed all who stood there. Not even an eyebrow moved as every person held their breath and looked on in horror with wide, unblinking eyes. The only sounds were the low threatening growls coming from the cheetahs. Everything else was silenced while Wosret lay there, his eyes glazed with fear and his hands and legs spread stiffly against the hard, tiled floor.

Then the cheetah at Wosret's throat snarled and lowered his head so that its fangs touched against the flesh of his neck.

Wosret's eyes were tightly closed now. His jaw rigid. Except for the small rise and fall of his chest, he lay as someone already dead. The silence seemed interminable.

It was Nefertiti who recovered first. She made a soft sound in the back of her throat. Everyone tensed. They knew she had only to give the command and Wosret's life would end. Kiya saw Nefertiti exchange glances with Amenhotep. Something precise seemed to pass between them without either speaking. Then Nefertiti nodded as if a decision had been made.

She snapped her fingers. 'Come here, you two!' Both cheetahs raised their heads and swung their gaze to look back at her, their paws still resting heavily against Wosret. The deep growling coming from their mouths eventually became a rumbling purr, until their chests and bodies heaved with the sound of it. Then, slowly and languidly, they rose from their crouched positions and stood on either side of Wosret, their lips pulled back, staring unblinkingly around the room as if loath to leave their prey.

Nefertiti stepped forward and looked down at Wosret in triumph. With the toe of her sandal she flicked her foot against the cheetahs' haunches. 'Come on now! Enough! Leave this man alone. There are tastier meals to be had. His flesh is probably poisoned with the venom of his evil ways. He's not worth eating.'

As the cheetahs turned and padded quietly to her side an audible sigh could be heard as everyone breathed out again.

It took a while longer for life to flow back into Wosret. He opened his eyes slowly and raised his hands to explore his throat as if checking that his neck was intact. Then he got to his feet and stood stiffly, not taking a step forward or backward, and spoke through tight lips. 'You'll regret this day you allowed your animals to threaten the Highest of High Priests of not only Thebes, but all Egypt.' He swept his gaze between Amenhotep and Nefertiti. 'You might be King and Queen but you're mere figureheads. Remember it was *I* who appointed you both and *I* who control Egypt and *I* who hold the power. The priests of Amun can't be pushed aside. The two of you won't spoil my plans. I have the power to silence *all* who get in my way . . . just as I silenced Tuthmosis.'

Amenhotep stepped forward. 'So it's *true*! You

ordered Samut to kill my brother. All that Princess Tadukhepa has told us is true.'

Wosret shrugged and looked triumphantly around the hall. 'No one can prove it.'

'Princess Tadukhepa's maid and Isikara will testify against you, and Samut will as well.'

Wosret shook his head. 'You're too late! You'll not find them. Neither the girls nor Samut. They've already been dealt with.'

'Dealt with?' Kiya gasped as she stepped forward. 'What have you done with Ta-Miu and Isikara?'

Nefertiti's eyes glittered. 'I won't *ever* regret the day I allowed my cheetahs to attack you. But I *will* regret not letting them finish the job.'

CHAPTER THIRTY-TWO

THE LABYRINTH

There was a moment of silence as Isikara and I stood before the gate of the labyrinth not knowing what would happen next. Then I wrenched myself free of the guard. 'Who has ordered this? Why are we being held captive? And why are we here at the labyrinth? I demand an answer.'

'Demand?' the guard sneered. 'You aren't in a position to demand anything.'

'Don't you know who we are? I'm maid to the Princess Tadukhepa, who is one of the King's wives and my friend is Isikara, daughter of the Priest at the Temple of Sobek.'

He glanced across at a fellow guard and shrugged. 'The names mean nothing to us.'

I gave him a look. He was more boy than man, with a fuzzy growth of hair sprouting from above his top lip. 'Surely the King means something to you!'

The guard shrugged. 'We take our orders not from the King but from the Highest of High Priests. He ordered us to bring you here.'

'Wosret?' I caught the look in Isikara's eyes.

The guard nodded at me. 'Now unlock the gate.'

I bit my lip, trying to think of anything that would delay us. 'Find the duplicate key!'

'You know that's gone. Stolen from the shelf by your friend.' He twisted my arm behind my back. 'Now hand over yours.'

'If I don't?'

'You'll regret it,' he sneered. 'But I think it won't be all you'll regret today. Now stop delaying.' His fingers gripped the cord around my neck and pulled. I felt it cut into my flesh. He bent close to my ear. 'Hand over the key or this nice little neck of yours might just be throttled. Do you hear me?'

'Give it to him, Ta-Miu,' Isikara urged.

As I removed the cord from my neck and handed him the key, he smiled. 'That's better.' He twisted it in the lock and the gate swung open, then he pushed us inside and followed close behind.

'My key.' I held out my hand. 'Give it back!'

A small twitch of amusement crossed his lips. 'Feisty, aren't you? You're not getting it back. It's ours now unless you can persuade me otherwise.' He ran his arm around my waist and cupped his hand beneath my breast and pulled me close towards him, so close I could smell his beery breath.

'Let go of me!' I jabbed my elbow into his ribs.

He glanced between the two of us and winked at the other guard. 'This is your last chance to have some fun. We're all alone here, just the four of us. You might as well enjoy these last moments. Give us a kiss, then.'

Isikara wrenched herself free from her guard and swung her fist into the shoulder of the one holding me. 'You heard her! Let go of her, you oaf!'

'Oaf, is it?' He leered up close to Isikara and I thought he would hit her.

His words still echoed in my head. 'Last moments? What do you mean?'

'Put it this way,' he sneered. 'You've seen your last ray of sunshine.'

'Don't speak in riddles!' Isikara snarled.

'Mind your tongue, girl!' He reached out to grab hold of her. 'We're taking you to King Amenhotep's burial chamber.'

I felt my breath catch. 'Why?'

'Why do people get taken to burial chambers?' A small smirk crossed his face as he watched us staring at him. He nodded. 'Yes, I think you're beginning to understand. You're going on a journey.'

'A journey?'

'A journey to the Afterlife. You're going to die. It's as simple as that!'

I heard Isikara's sharp gasp. 'Why?'

'Wosret commands it.'

I shook my head. 'You don't have to do everything Wosret commands.'

'Don't make this difficult. We've been given orders. We have to carry them out. I want to get home to my supper. But don't say I didn't try to make your last while in this world a little happier.' He planted a kiss on Isikara's neck. 'Maybe you can persuade your friend there's still a chance for some fun.'

'Fun? With either of you? We'd rather drink poison!' Isikara spat the words out as she furiously wiped the place on her neck.

'Oh would you? Well, you might *long* for poison instead of the end chosen for you.'

The end? I looked across at Isikara. Her face reflected what I'm sure mine showed. We were both too terrified to ask.

'What do you say?' He turned to the other guard. 'Shall we force them to have some fun?'

The other guard shook his head. 'Leave them be. I want to get home. They're too scrawny in any case. I like my girls fleshy. I'd rather hurry up and get home to my own girl. These ones are too grand for me. Putting on airs and graces as if they're Nefertiti themselves. I can't bear the likes of them. Let's hurry with what we have to do.'

'Just one little kiss.' My guard grabbed hold of me and pushed me hard against the wall. So hard, I felt the knobs of my spine against the rock. Then he gripped my hands above my head and pressed his mouth against my lips.

'Leave her!'

It was a man's voice. Suddenly the outline of two figures appeared in the gateway. I narrowed my eyes to focus against the light. One was definitely a guard and the other was . . .? Could it be? Had he come to save us?

'*Samut!*' I called out.

Beside me I heard Isikara's quick intake of breath. 'Samut?'

'It's him all right!' the guard sneered. 'But don't get any ideas. He's not here to save you. His fate is the same as yours. Get along with you now.'

Before I had a chance to speak, the one with the sprouting top lip pushed me forward. 'Walk. We've waited too long for this other fellow. We've no more time to waste now.' He pulled the gate sharply shut behind Samut and his guard, and twisted the key in the lock and slipped it into his girdle bag. 'Get going now!' Then he took the lamp the other guard had lit and held it so that the light flickered ahead into the darkness.

Isikara glared at him. 'The labyrinth is vast. Do you know exactly where you're going?'

The guard grinned back at her. 'Yes. And I know you've been here before. You helped Tuthmosis. Now see where it's got you!' He nodded his head towards Samut. 'And he knows the way too. So we won't be getting lost!'

'I don't regret helping Tuthmosis. And you haven't answered.'

'We're going to the well that blocks the passageway leading into the King's burial chamber.'

'The well?' Isikara looked across at me. I felt my eyes widen. I knew about the well. It had smooth sides and no footholds and was deep. Yes, we both knew. I felt my throat close up and fought to fill my lungs with air as if I was already drowning.

300

Isikara managed a scornful look. 'Water doesn't bother me. I'm a good swimmer.'

'A good swimmer! Hah! Not when there's no river-bank to swim to. No footholds to help you out. Just slippery sides that will keep you in there going around and around like a rat trying to get out of a beer vat.'

Words dried up in my throat. The labyrinth ceiling seemed to push down on me. I could hardly draw breath. Isikara might be a good swimmer. She'd lived all her life next to the Great River. But I wasn't. When Kiya and I came from Mitanni, the horsemen had carried us across the rivers on their horses and at the deepest places the horses had swum with us desperately clinging to their necks. I would drown the moment I was thrown into the well. I wouldn't last as long as a rat.

And *why*? All because of Samut. Samut, who was walking in silence behind us.

We were passing through a confusion of passage-ways that twisted this way and that, with enormous paintings of gods and doorways and archways that led to more and more rooms. At times Anubis glared down at us and at other times Amenhotep. And once Nut was above, sprinkling gold stars down on us from the vaulted ceiling. But it was all a blur. Even some creature scuttling across my foot meant nothing. My body was numb. I felt as if a thousand scorpions had stung me and my legs shuffled forward without knowing how.

I lost all points of reference. Perhaps we were lost. Eventually, when it seemed we had come to a dead-end, one of the guards stepped ahead of us. He placed both palms against the stone wall. My eyes searched the gloom. Where were we? I held my breath. For a moment nothing happened and then an entire segment of wall swung open and shifted inward into a dark cavity.

A creature seemed to leap out at us but it was a stone statue of Anubis with eyes that blazed in the lamplight. My heartbeat quickened as we stepped past it through the opening into a passageway which led into a vast hall. A ceiling stretched high above us and mysterious alcoves and passageways led away from the lamplight into utter blackness. Instead of being hot and stuffy, a cool waft of air brushed across my face. The echoing sound of our footsteps and the voices of the guards told how huge the space was.

'Be careful of how you tread!' Isikara whispered up close to me.

My guard lifted his lamp high. 'There, that's it.' He nodded. 'The well.'

I glanced down. Suddenly my insides dropped from me. Right at our feet, in a sharp bend of passageway taking up the whole width, was a deep shaft with sides of solid, smooth rock. A long, narrow stone slab lay stretched across it, put there by someone ... perhaps even Samut when he was last in the tomb. Far, far below, the lamplight flickered against an oily black sheen of water.

The guard nodded again. 'It's deep.' He didn't have to say more. He picked up a small pebble from the stone floor and dropped it. There was a long, drawn-out moment of silence. When my ears felt they could stand it no longer, I finally heard the splash.

'*Very* deep!' He looked across at Isikara. 'No matter how good a swimmer you are.'

She shrugged. 'What harm have we done you? Do you always follow Wosret's orders so blindly like goats being led to the slaughtering post?'

I bit my lip, thinking she'd used the wrong comparison. It was the three of us who were the goats being led to slaughter. When I glanced across at Samut he wouldn't meet my eye.

'Shut your mouth!' a guard snapped at Isikara but she was not to be stopped.

'Can't you show you are men and not mere boys?'

I saw the loathing and derision in her glance.

303

'Men stand up for themselves and make their own decisions about what is right or wrong. You know this is wrong. You know we're innocent.'

'That may be so, but *he's* not.' Samut's guard gave him a shake. 'He murdered Tuthmosis.'

Samut flung off his guard's hold and spoke for the first time. 'I murdered him for a reason.'

I looked across at him, scared for all of us by the strange look in his eyes. A wild sweep of his arms, one quick movement, and he could've grabbed any one of us and pushed us into the well, or jumped and pulled us with him. I tried to keep my voice very quiet and calm. 'Why, Samut?'

'*Why?*' His eyes blazed. 'Because I hated both of them. Him *and* his father. They took the only thing I truly loved away from me.'

'What?'

'The horses.'

The horses? I thought back to my evenings with him at the stables. Of course.

'I was a stable hand when Tuthmosis fell from his father's chariot and crushed his leg. Afterwards the accident was blamed on me. The King said I hadn't harnessed his horses properly. I would *never* have neglected to do that. But no one believed me. The King demanded my job be taken from me.'

'Tuthmosis never blamed his lameness on you.' Isikara's voice was calm but hard. 'He never mentioned your name. He told me it was an accident. He said they'd been travelling too fast. That the wheel hit a stone and he was jolted from the chariot and fell with his leg crushed under by the weight of it.'

'But his father blamed me. He was King. And Tuthmosis would've been as well. I hated them both for taking what I loved most away from me. I couldn't get work in any stable after that.'

'You can't hate someone who's innocent. Tuthmosis probably didn't even know you'd lost your job.' I saw Isikara clench her fists as if she had to prevent herself from giving Samut a hard push so that he'd fall backwards into the well.

'Exactly. He didn't care. I was just the stable boy. But I suffered. And all the riches I stole from this tomb were only so I could disrupt the King's journey to the Afterlife. I wanted the King punished. I didn't care anything for the jewels and gold. I gave it all away.'

I tried to catch his glance. 'Did you care for me?'

Samut looked away.

'Samut?' I asked again.

'I did once, but the ankh around your neck reminded me that Tuthmosis was your first love.'

305

Isikara swept a look around us all. 'And now here we are and we must decide what must be done.'

Done? I looked across at her. Had she suddenly gone mad? Why was she hurrying our end, reminding the guards of what they were meant to be doing?

She nodded. 'Surely we can decide this together.'

Her guard shook his head and laughed. 'What's to decide? The decision's already made. We're to see that the three of you are thrown into the well. Wosret commands it.'

Isikara laughed as if she thought him a fool. 'That's a stupid idea and you know it! Why would you commit such a crime in such a sacred place? And for that matter, why would you want to turn the well sour with our bodies? King Amenhotep's spirit would never rest. He'd never leave you in peace. And when the three of you in turn die, and it's time for you to travel on the Ferry-Boat of Ra to the World of the Dead, Thoth will be waiting for you in the Hall of Maat with the Scales of Justice and will ask, *Why have you come?*

'What will you answer? *My heart is righteous*, is what he wants to hear. *I am pure. I have done no evil in place of right and truth.* But will any of you be able to say it? Will you be able to speak or will your jaws clamp shut? When Anubis's eyes glow like burning coals and Ammut bears her teeth and her snout is bloody, will you be able to say *I have not disobeyed the gods. I have not inflicted pain on anyone. I have not killed*, so when your hearts are placed on the Scales of Justice, yours will rise lighter than a feather? I don't think so! If you throw us down the well, there'll be no truth in your words.'

The guard holding her shrugged as he looked around at the other two. 'I've had enough of her. Let's shut her up for good! She can be the *first* to go!'

Samut took a step forward. 'No! Push me in first. I'm not scared to die. Go on!' he challenged.

But my guard, the one with fuzz on his lip, was wide-eyed. 'Wait. She's right you know. We won't be able to answer.'

This was all Isikara needed. She plunged straight on as if she hadn't been interrupted, without pausing for breath. 'The answer to all this is, *no!* No, you won't be able to say any of these things. And Ammut will snatch your hearts and drag them off. Is that how you want your lives to end?'

'Stop wasting time. Let me shut her up. Her words are making me prickly, as if Ammut's breath is already on my neck.'

'*You* do it then, if you're so anxious to shut her up.'

'Isikara . . .' I pulled her arm. Tried to stop her ranting.

But she took no notice. Her eyes flicked over them. 'You are all fools. Do you want all three of our deaths on your hands just because Wosret demands it? Which of you will be brave enough to shove the first of us in?'

I squeezed my eyes shut. Held my breath. No sound came. No one moved.

'He's the Highest of High Priests, how can we refuse him?' It was my guard speaking.

'Enough, now!' Samut's guard nudged his friend. 'She has far too much to say. Let's take action.'

'Or you could leave us here,' Isikara went on, her voice calm, not pleading, just firm. In the lamplight she looked innocent. But I knew better. It was a trap. She was playing a game as subtle and tactical as a board game where an unsuspecting opponent is urged to make a move that will help her own piece reach the other side unscathed. 'Go back and say you've done the deed. Imagine how much better you'll sleep tonight. Innocent of murder. Later we'll escape. We'll all three leave Thebes and never return. No one will bother to search for our bodies in the well. No one will ever know.'

She made it seem so simple. Her words were quiet

and persuasive, as if anyone could have thought of it, even the guards if they'd given themselves enough time. She was almost suggesting it was their idea in the first place.

'No one will know and you'll be innocent of murder. When you stand in front of Thoth your hearts will rest lightly on the Scales of Justice. Thoth will reward you. Don't you believe any wise man would do this?'

No one spoke. The dark spaces were silent except for the echo of her words that hung in the air.

'No! Enough delaying!' Her guard jostled her forward.

I heard the sound of my voice echoing through the spaces as I screamed. Then everything happened too fast to understand the order. Samut's arm went up. His fist struck straight at Isikara's guard's chin so that he was flung back and hit the stone floor with a dull thud.

Run!' Samut shouted at us. But we had turned to stone. Samut had already spun around and came thumping into the stomach of the second guard. He too fell to the floor with a huge gasp of air leaving his body.

The third guard sprang at Samut, knocking them both to the ground where they lay fighting with their fists. Then suddenly the guard managed to pull free. He jumped up and stood facing all three of us. Isikara wrenched me back from the edge of the well. But it was Samut he lunged at. Samut sidestepped. The guard slipped and suddenly he overbalanced and began falling. And as he did, he thrust out a hand and grabbed and took Samut with him into the well.

With a terrible scream they both disappeared over the edge into the darkness. Then a long moment of silence. Afterwards the splashes, much louder than the sound of a stone, as the two bodies hit the water.

I stood paralysed. I couldn't bear to look over the edge and see both men so far down in that dark, oily water fighting for their lives, until each was too tired to keep their heads above the surface. But Isikara grabbed hold of the lamp that was on the floor and stepped forward.

'He's dead.' A muffled gasp came up to us as if from the end of a long tunnel. 'He must've hit his head against the side as he fell.'

It was Samut's voice.

CHAPTER THIRTY-THREE

THE RETURN

I stood back, hardly daring to breathe. Watched Isikara looking down at Samut. Imagined his face pale in the lamplight far below. I waited for her to speak. But she said nothing. The moment seemed very long. I could hear the sound of Samut splashing.

Then Isikara turned and eyed me. 'Which guard has your key?'

I stared wide-eyed back at her. The key! We needed the key. The duplicate one inside the gate had been stolen by Samut, my guard had said. Why else had he wanted the key from around my neck?

I looked around desperately. Was it my guard who had fallen into the well? But no, I suddenly remembered he was the youngest one. The one with the fuzzy lip who Isikara had almost persuaded. I searched the two faces of the prone bodies and then flung myself at him.

The key was still in his girdle bag. I held it up.

'Hurry! There's not a moment to lose.' Isikara grabbed my hand and without looking back we ran past the statue of Anubis into the labyrinth.

Neither of us said his name. Neither of us spoke. We hurried away. My breath coming in huge gasps. The sound of our feet slapping against the stone. The thought of light at the end of the labyrinth pulling me forward. The deep, dark well behind us pulling me back. The questions storming inside me.

My body suddenly seemed heavy. My legs slowed down beneath me as if someone had tied stones to them. I stopped and saw Isikara had stopped as well. She looked at me.

What? What are you looking at? I wanted to yell at her.

But we stood there silent as stone, arms at our sides, each with our own thoughts swirling around and around. Not looking at each other any more. Facing forward with the darkness and terror at our back.

Samut splashing around and around in the oily, black water.

He would truly die. Get weaker and weaker. Sink into the water. Then darkness. Then nothing.

I felt my eyes stretching wider and wider. *We can't just leave him*, is what I wanted to shout. I knew I had to turn back.

Isikara looked at me. In the lamplight a shadow seemed to pass over her face. We both turned. Started walking back. Then, running. Isikara pulling me along so that our breath came in gasps.

At the edge of the well I squeezed my eyes shut. Hung back. Folded myself into the darkness. Held my breath. Listened to the hollow silence. Just the sound of our breath. No sound of water now. He had surely drowned already.

But he was still alive. 'Samut! Samut!' I heard Isikara call urgently. 'Keep swimming, Samut! We'll be back soon.' Then she turned to me. 'Quick! Follow me!' She crossed onto the stone slab that lay across the well's opening and held the lamp up high.

'Come on, Ta-Miu!'

I stared down at the water as I stepped onto the narrow slab and tried to force my feet forward. Far below I could see Samut's face staring up, pale as a moon in the darkness. All I could think of was that deep, dark water and how cold it would be to sink under it forever.

'Step across, Ta-Miu! You *have* to! There's no time to waste. Stop looking down. Look at me.' She held her hand out and grabbed me as I collapsed against her. 'Quick!' She pulled me down some steps into a long passage that led into a vast chamber with a ceiling that disappeared into darkness. In the middle of the vault was a huge stone sarcophagus . . . King Amenhotep's surely? But there was no time to get my bearings. Isikara pulled me into a side chamber. In the lamplight everything glittered. Heaps of chariots lay piled in a corner. Statues of gold stared back. Caskets lay open with jewels scattered across the floor.

'Where are we?' My voice came out in a strange, hoarse whisper.

'King Amenhotep's storage chamber for his Afterlife.' She started pulling things, flinging open caskets and rummaging. 'Find any length of material that's strong. There must be something in here we can use. Pray that Samut knocked out those guards well enough and they don't come around too soon. And pray Samut manages to keep swimming.'

'What are we going to do?'

'Pull him up, of course!' She grabbed a bundle of cloth stacked up in a far corner. 'Here. Take a few. We might have to tie them together. Hurry!'

But I stood looking at her. 'Why?'

'Why what?'

'Why're you doing this? Why are you rescuing him? Samut murdered the person you loved.'

Isikara twitched her shoulders as if something prickly had fallen down her back. 'Should we murder the person you loved? We have to do what's right.'

I could hear Samut's splashes even before we reached the well.

'Praise Hathor,' Isikara breathed. 'He's still alive.' She called down. 'Samut! We've got cloth. We're going to pull you up.'

She grabbed a length and tied a knot around the base of the statue of Anubis. 'That'll help anchor him in case we slip.'

Slip? Might we slip in? My heart thumped in my throat as I peered down the well.

Isikara hurled the other end of the cloth into the well. 'A pestilence! It doesn't reach. Quick. Hand me another length,' she said as she pulled it back up.

My hands were shaking as I tied a knot to join the two pieces. The guard right next to us was rolling his eyes and moaning and looked as if he might come round at any moment.

We could have gone. We might have made it in time. We could have run for the labyrinth gate.

Escaped. Just the two of us. Isikara and I. But neither of us could have left Samut. Isikara had escaped this tomb once already. With Tuthmosis. But now she would escape it with his murderer.

She was ripping off her sandals. She nodded. 'Take yours off as well. To give more grip.' She flung the end of the cloth down. 'Can you reach it? Are you ready, Samut?' Her voice echoed into the well. 'Lever your feet against the sides as we pull.'

She nodded at me. I was in front with her at my back. My shoulders felt as if they were ripping from my flesh as we took the full burden of him. I felt my feet losing their grip. Slipping forward. Please, Horus, don't let the cloth tear. Don't let us fall in. Then suddenly the burden lessened as Samut rose above the water and took some of his weight with his feet against the walls.

'Find any ridge to give you grip,' Isikara shouted.

We could hear Samut grunting with his efforts.

'Step back! Step back!' Isikara shouted close to my ear. 'You'll fall in!'

I looked down. My feet were just a pace away from the edge of the well. I pulled with all my strength. Suddenly a hand gripped the edge.

'Help him, Ta-Miu, while I keep holding.'

Then there were two hands on the edge and his face

appeared, his legs scrabbling against the edge while I tried to grip his slippery shoulders and ease him over onto the floor.

For a moment our eyes locked. Then he gripped my hand and fell forward at my feet. Wet. Slimy with muck. Exhausted.

'Quick now, Samut.' Isikara reached down to help. 'There's no time to recover. We have to run for it. You knocked the guards out well enough. But they'll recover soon.'

Samut stared back at us, no life left in his eyes. 'There's no point.'

'What?'

'What's the point of me coming with you? I'll meet my end in any case. I'm doomed if I return. And doomed if I stay locked in here.'

'Stop wasting time. Come on!'

Still he held back.

I looked across at him, suddenly annoyed. 'Do you think we did all this so we could have you arrested and put to death?'

'Why else?'

'Why would we risk our lives to save you? We could've escaped easily.'

'Come on now, Samut,' Isikara said briskly. 'We're taking you back to bear witness against Wosret.

That'll be your protection. And the fact that you helped us. Stood by us. You have my word.'

Then we all three stumbled forward through the labyrinth. Stumbled out of the dark winding passages into the shining light of Thebes.

The sun blazed down and blinded our eyes. The great chalky cliff rising up behind us and the green valley with the wide river below shivered in brightness. Shimmered and glimmered as never before.

We were free. We had escaped the labyrinth. We had escaped death.

Who would have believed the three of us could feel such happiness? Even as the mud and slime dried and cracked against our skins and faces, we looked at each other and laughed. And would have thrown ourselves down in the grass and gasped huge gulps of air, had we not been in such a hurry.

We had never known such light, such air, such perfume, such freedom as that afternoon as we ran through the fields of Thebes away from the darkness of the tomb.

Epilogue

We entered the Great Hall with the muck of the labyrinth still stuck to us. All eyes turned towards us. Even the attendants stood goggle-eyed as we paused in the doorway. They looked at us standing there, covered in mud and slime, as if we were creatures crawled back from the Afterlife. They had believed us dead. And now we had returned as spirits.

But as we walked forward, Isikara, Samut and I, our bare feet leaving muddy footprints across the pattern of herons and lotus lilies that floated across the floor, we knew differently. We'd come back from the edge of darkness that had threatened to swallow us. But we were real. We were alive. As alive as any of them standing goggle-eyed and gawping in the Great Hall.

It was Isikara who spoke first. And even then her voice was firm. She bowed and addressed Amenhotep and Nefertiti. 'We've come back from the labyrinth. We've brought Samut back as well.' She said no more but I knew it was Wosret that her words were meant for. She was daring him to speak.

All eyes turned to him. But for once the silence held. Wosret's words had dried up in the back of his throat.

Isikara took Samut's hand and guided him forward. 'We brought him back so justice can be done. Listen to his story and you will know where the real evil lies.'

Then Nefertiti and Amenhotep heard the true story of all that had happened from the time of Tuthmosis's chariot accident to the time of his poisoning by Wosret and finally to the time of Tuthmosis's death. And justice was done.

Thebes was deserted and rebuilt further north along the Great River at Amarna where the Priests of Amun lost their power to the Sun-God, Aten. There, in the splendour of Amarna, where art and beauty abounded, Amenhotep ruled as King unchallenged until his death, and changed his name from Amenhotep to Akhenaten to reflect his love of Aten. And there Nefertiti bore her first child, a daughter named Meritaten, and afterwards five more beautiful daughters . . . but no son . . . and became a loving and devoted mother.

And there at Amarna Isikara became a high priestess of Aten, the God of Light, and was no longer haunted by the image of the Great Crocodile God, Sobek, rising up to tear her apart. And in Amarna Samut was reinstated at the new stables with its magnificent chariot-racing arena where he became the finest horse-trainer ever known in the Kingdom of Egypt. And there Ta-Miu, true to her heritage, employed all the knowledge and skills she had learnt from her father and brothers in Mitanni and worked side by side with Samut, the first woman ever to be employed in the royal stables ... but not the first woman to drive her own chariot!

And in Amarna Kiya grew more and more radiant and had a sun-court especially erected for her ... where no doubt she kept chameleons ... and caused the only small ripple in the peace of the new Palace when she bore Amenhotep a son. His *only* son. The son's name was Tutankhaten, who renamed himself Tutankhamun after the old god, Amun.

And as for Wosret? The history of Wosret is unrecorded. He disappeared. Some say he was made to drink poison that day in the Great Hall. Some say the cheetahs were called to take their revenge. Others say his death was cunningly devised by Nefertiti. That she had him thrown to the sacred crocodiles that he'd so neglected at the Temple of Sobek. And in so doing, she condemned him to the worst death of all ... one where his body was never mummified so that his spirit could never be reunited with his body in the Afterlife.

But whatever end came to him, it's clear that his name was erased from the history of Egypt. No sign will be found of him or his name on any building, amulet or wig box, and no statue will be found, even toppled in the desert sand, nor any mummy buried deep in the labyrinth of the chalk-stone mountains of Thebes. The subterranean passages have housed mummies of kings and commoners and creatures from bulls to baboons and crocodiles to cats. There is even said to be a lion burial ground in homage to the fighting spirit of the goddess Sekhmet somewhere out in the sands of the desert that has never been excavated.

But no mummy will *ever* be found of Wosret.

Justice was done.

AUTHOR'S NOTE

The title, *Eye of the Sun*, comes from the Eye of Horus, the Egyptian Falcon God. The all-seeing eye was believed to have healing powers and was used as a protective amulet. The right eye of Horus represented the sun and the Sun God. The mirror image, or left eye, represented the moon and the God Thoth. The ancient Egyptians believed that spiritually, the right eye reflected solar, masculine energy and ruled reason and mathematics while the left eye reflected fluid, feminine, lunar energy and ruled intuition and magic. Together, they represented the combined power of Horus and the whole of the universe.

The catalyst for both *Eye of the Moon* and *Eye of the Sun* was a double-page spread of three mutilated mummies splashed across a Sunday paper. One of the mummies was believed to be Queen Tiy, the grandmother of Tutankhamen. Next to her was a young boy, supposedly her son, Tuthmosis, and alongside him, a mummy that was possibly Nefertiti, '*The Beautiful*', who became the wife of Tiy's second son, Amenhotep.

Murder, mystery and intrigue are part of the history of Ancient Egypt. Why were the mummies sealed up in a tiny insignificant chamber and why were they mutilated? And why in particular was the mouth of Nefertiti, one of Egypt's most compelling and mysterious of figures, smashed with such obvious intent? Was it to prevent her from speaking out in the Afterlife?

My first encounter with Nefertiti was in the Agyptisches Museum in Berlin in June 1990, seven months after the fall of the Berlin Wall. The city was in a state of euphoria, yet inside the museum, Nefertiti, with her long elegant neck and chiselled beauty, seemed cool, aloof and removed from the uproar outside. She had known similar turmoil coming to the throne at the age of about fourteen, with the city of Thebes, known as Waset then, in an uproar. Her young husband, Amenhotep, was overthrowing the old order of worship and abandoning all Egyptian deities in favour of a single god, the sun itself – Aten.

And as I stood staring at her through her case of polished glass, three thousand years later, it was easy to imagine what power this enigmatic Egyptian

Pharaoh-Queen must have had over her subjects . . . and easy to imagine her many admirers but also her many enemies.